ONE STEP TOO FAR

Claire Escott had ignored her father's warning against involvement with her fiancé, Mark Rowland. However, she little realised the extent of the scientist's corroding ambition. And it was not long after their marriage that Rowland's ruthless pursuit of a scientific empire encompassed a horrifying murder. But that was only the start of things. Mark's scientific genius and obsessive ambition to go one step further eventually led to mass destruction — and the ultimate sacrifice . . .

JOHN RUSSELL FEARN

ONE STEP TOO FAR

Complete and Unabridged

LINFORD
Leicester

First published in Great Britain

First Linford Edition
published 2008

British Library CIP Data

Fearn, John Russell, *1908 – 1960*
    One step too far.—Large print ed.—
Linford mystery library
1. Ambition—Fiction 2. Scientists—Fiction
3. Suspense fiction 4. Large type books
I. Title
823.9′12 [F]

ISBN 978–1–84782–219–2

Published by
F. A. Thorpe (Publishing)
Anstey, Leicestershire

Set by Words & Graphics Ltd.
Anstey, Leicestershire
Printed and bound in Great Britain by
T. J. International Ltd., Padstow, Cornwall

This book is printed on acid-free paper

1

Dangerous ambition

To his fellow workers, and the world in general, Mark Rowland was a radio-television technician. Employed by the World Broadcasting Company — the W.B.C. — of London, he filled an important, even if not greatly publicised position as resident maintenance engineer, and he knew his job. In fact he was a specialist at it. There had been times when the cleverest radio engineers in the world had consulted him, and he had never failed to solve a problem.

There was nothing miraculous about his ability. He was no super-genius of radio-television, but he had certainly spent all his time since being about ten years of age improving his mind upon this specialized line — radio-television, and its many ramifications. Now, at thirty, he was prepared to put a lifetime's study to the test.

For there was a side to Mark Rowland known only to two people — Claire Escott, his fiancée, and Ted Shepley, his best friend. Claire, Mark's main interest, had the intelligence to appreciate that Mark knew what he was talking about and always did her best to encourage him — though perhaps, since he was a young man with devouring ambition it would have been better if she'd refrained. In these days of comparative youth she did not appreciate the lengths to which Mark might go with sufficient incentive.

It was on a warm June evening when Mark revealed the 'other side' to his apparently humdrum life. He had met Claire by pre-arrangement in Regent's Park — it being his night off from the W.B.C. — and at first they merely exchanged the pleasantries of any engaged couple as they strolled along in the evening warmth; then presently Claire began to sense that her husband-to-be was labouring under extreme tension. She looked at him curiously.

'Anything the matter, Mark?' She hugged more tightly the arm with which he held her. 'You're like a bomb about to explode.'

'Just how I feel,' he smiled; and did not explain immediately.

Claire did not press the matter, knowing he would talk when he was ready. They continued walking — she smallish and blonde in her matter-of-fact summer two-piece; and he tall, gaunt, and somewhat untidy. There was a generous ugliness about him which most people liked. His mouth was large, his nose hooked, and his eyes a penetrating grey. Redemption lay in the sweep of his forehead and his direct speech. He always knew what he meant, and said so.

'There's a seat,' he said abruptly, nodding. 'Time we rested.'

Claire nodded rather meekly and they made their way to it and settled down. For a moment or two Mark was silent, his long legs thrust out in front of him, arms folded, his eyes watching gambolling children under the trees in the distance.

'It won't be long now, Claire, before we can marry,' he said at length, glancing at her.

'That's hardly news, Mark. Certainly it doesn't explain why you're marching around like Napoleon before launching a victorious offensive.'

He ignored the levity in her tone — or else did not notice it. He had no humour in his make-up.

'What makes our marriage a certainty is a discovery I have made which will net a fortune,' he explained. 'Up to now I have been making the excuse of lack of finance the reason for our remaining engaged.'

Claire's hazel eyes studied him frankly. He was not looking at her now. She only saw his lean, powerful profile, a white collar that was soiled, a necktie on the slant, and a tweed jacket ready for dry cleaning.

'Sooner we get married, the better,' she said.

'You've been wondering for a long time why I've pleaded shortage of funds I suppose. You haven't said so openly, but you must have thought it.'

'Well, I — I know you must get well paid,' Claire admitted.

'I do — reasonably well, but every cent

4

has been ploughed back into private experiments, and now they're going to pay a big dividend. The man with the original ideas makes the fortunes, Claire, and I have the most original idea of the present decade.'

'Oh . . . ' Claire waited whilst he brooded. 'And — and what is it? Or can't you tell me?'

At this he turned to look at her. 'Outside of a very trusted friend, you are the first person to know of this discovery. You would have been really the first, only it demanded a scientist in partnership with me. To sum up briefly, I've carried radio-television to its ultimate possibility — or nearly ultimate, depending on later investigations — and have transmitted a block of cooking salt from here to Brighton.'

If Mark's manner had not been so serious, his grey eyes so piercing whilst he spoke, Claire would have laughed out-right. The science went right over her head and all she saw was the cooking salt. Even as it was a smile quirked her pretty mouth.

'It isn't funny,' Mark stated flatly.

'I'm sure it isn't meant to be, Mark, but — What does it achieve? Is it revolutionary?'

'It is revolutionary insofar that the block of salt was never visible as a block of salt during its journey. It was electronic waves, and nothing else.'

'Now you're being scientific. I haven't the least idea what you're talking about.'

Mark hunched closer. 'It's radio-television in a new form. Or, if it is simpler for you to grasp, it is like radio transmission, only instead of transmitting sounds — or vision in the case of television — I transmit inorganic compounds.'

Dimly Claire began to see the point. She caught her breath slightly.

'But, Mark, how on earth can you?'

'Well the actual scientific details would turn you dizzy, so I'd better water them down for you. In radio, the original sounds are broken down into electronic waves, distributed electromagnetically, and re-built up in the receiver into the original sounds.

'All right then. In television we get much the same thing — the breaking down of the original into electronic patterns, the distribution to a distance, and the reassembly into the original scene or picture. Now, for long enough, I've believed that if we can transmit sound and vision over a distance we ought also to be able to transmit solids. And that is what I have done, the experimental solid being a block of cooking salt. I chose that because at any vibration affecting it the salt would break up. But it didn't. It arrived under the receiver in Brighton still in its maker's wrapping. A perfect example of solid transmission over fifty miles!'

'To call it marvellous is an understatement,' Claire said, 'but I still don't see how you do it.'

'I simply use radio methods, with variations. I break down the object electrically into its atomic make-up or pattern. In this form it is held in what is called an 'electronic parcel' by means of magnetic forces; then it is 'transmitted' by the ordinary radio electronic process and picked up by the receiver at a given distance. Distance is governed by the power of dissemination used. At the receiving end the 'parcel' is undone and reformed into its original atomic make-up. The material pattern reforms identically, of course, and there you are. It is all scientific, accurate, and the outcome of years of trial and error in experiment.'

Even now Claire could not altogether understand. Most certainly she did not realize that Mark Rowland had accomplished something ranking in importance, and possible future development, with the experiments of Marconi, Tesla, and other pioneers of radio. Nor did she see that in sending a block of salt unharmed to Brighton Mark had repeated, on a grander scale, the success of Marconi when he had sent a wireless signal across the Channel.

'Hasn't it registered?' Mark asked bluntly, after a while.

'Not altogether.' Claire gave a smile and laid a hand on his arm. 'I'm not much gifted scientifically, Mark. I suppose you'll sell the invention and that will be the dividend you were speaking of?'

'Sell it? Sell it!' Mark nearly hooted. 'Great heavens, no! I'm going to form a company and call it the Rowland Electronic-Transmission Company. I'll be the managing director, and you and Ted Shepley will be my co-directors. I'm putting all the money I can spare into it and so's Ted. If you wish to put cash in, okay. If not, all right. I thought you'd want to be cut in on it, though. This business is going to pay enormous dividends. I shan't be satisfied until I've run the air, land, and sea freight routes out of business. When I've got that far I'll really be something!'

Claire frowned. 'What has freight got to do with it?'

'Do you not understand, my dear, that anything — no matter what — can be transmitted by my process for any desired distance? What is more, the transmission takes place at the speed of light. One hundred and eighty-six thousand miles in a second. Instantaneous delivery to any point on the Earth! Think of that for business firms. Instant delivery! No more hold-ups. Weight and size doesn't signify.

Given enough power and big enough transmitters and receivers I could transplant the Empire State Building to the North Pole in an instant . . . That of course is wild exaggeration, but you see what I mean?'

'I believe I do,' Claire whispered, gazing before her.

'Once I get that established,' Mark went on tensely, 'I take the next step. The transmission of organic subjects — animals, and then human beings.'

'But you couldn't do it with living creatures, surely?'

'I shall before I'm finished.' Mark's big mouth set resolutely and for a moment Claire caught a glimpse of the burning ambition that animated him. She was not quite sure whether or not it frightened her, deep down.

'Who's Ted Shepley?' she asked, changing the subject.

'Ted? Why, my partner. Actually he's a ham radio enthusiast and I met him several years ago at a radio conference for amateurs. We got talking and things just grew. Clever in his way on the designing side, but he doesn't get the ideas. I'm the one who does that. At the moment he's on a holiday in Brighton. He's rented a small office on the outskirts of the town and in it is fixed up the receiver for my electronic transmitter. We're in constant touch by telephone.'

'And where's your transmitter?'

'I'm using an old, broken-down garage at the moment. I got it on a cheap rental right in the heart of the city. Nobody can break in and steal anything because I've electrified the walls.'

Claire started. 'But isn't that illegal? Like — like putting broken glass on top of a wall without permission?'

'Illegal, possibly. But I value my apparatus enough to take the risk, and I can't carry it about with me. Some of it I've bought. The rest I've . . . borrowed.' Mark hesitated for a moment.

'Borrowed? You don't mean stolen, do you?'

'I said borrowed!' Mark snapped. 'Anyway, it wasn't anything much — a cathode-ray tube, one or two off-standard transformers, some p.e.c. units . . . What's a few pounds to a crowd like the World Broadcasting Company?'

'Nothing, of course, only — ' Claire shrugged away the thought that presented itself to her and said, 'Probably dad will be interested in your invention. He'll understand it better anyway since at one time he was a consulting engineer — before he retired.'

'Possibly,' Mark admitted. 'He might even be willing to join the company. In fact I'm sure he will once he sees the possibilities. This thing is going to sweep the world Claire,' he continued, gesturing. 'In time it will supersede all other means of transit. The very speed of the business will convince those who must cut time to a minimum.'

'Unless the thought of being blown to atoms and then re-assembled, causes more to shy away than accept the idea,' Claire pointed out. 'As far as freight goes, though, I can definitely see the advantages — and I'm all for it. Now let's see what father has to say.'

She got to her feet purposefully and all the way back to her home, through the twilight, Mark talked of nothing but science and its immense scope. Nothing else was in his mind but the infinite possibilities of his discovery. Claire contented herself with 'Yes' and 'No', yet part of the time found herself thinking about the various pieces of equipment he had taken without permission. Was it theft or just overriding ambition that bent everything to the cause without thought of scruples? She wanted to see it the latter way for the obvious reason that she could not imagine her life without Mark. To him, though he had never admitted the fact even to himself, Claire was just a necessity in his life because she was a woman and because she tried to understand. Love was something Mark Rowland did not possess: he did not even love science; he just had a respect for it. Claire's father was a bluff, rosy-checked man of sixty odd, even-tempered and thoughtful. With Claire's mother, who very rarely had much to say, he inhabited a rambling old-style house on the outskirts of Hampstead. Indeed he was at the gate, smoking his pipe in the peaceful evening, as Mark and Claire came arm-in-arm along the avenue. 'Early for you two young ones, isn't it?' he asked, smiling, as they came up. 'Only ten fifteen!'

'With good reason, dad,' Claire said. 'Mark's got something to say to you.'

'So it's come at last?' Mr. Escott knocked the ashes from his pipe against the gatepost.

'No, not that,' Mark answered, saturnine as ever. 'That comes later. It's business — important business. Might turn you in a fortune. In fact it will. Ask Claire.'

'Sounds feasible to me,' Claire confirmed.

'Does it now? Well, m'dear, since you've never struck me as a brilliant business woman maybe we'd better have a chat. Come along inside.'

Coming inside meant indulging in a light supper and talking of irrelevancies whilst all the time Mark was itching to get to the point. To hurry the placid Mr. Escott was impossible, however. He only drifted around to the subject towards eleven-thirty when he was seated in his favourite armchair and his pipe drawing smoothly.

'It concerns freight, Mr. Escott,' Mark explained, and the very immensity of his subject kept him prowling around the lounge whilst Claire and her mother watched him from the settee.

'Freight?' Mr. Escott repeated, surprised. 'I always thought you were a television engineer.'

'I am — definitely. And that leads up to freight. Let me outline my discovery and then see what you think.'

So Mr. Escott listened without interrupting to very much the same theory that had been explained to his daughter, though on this occasion there were many technical elaborations.

'I insist that it can sweep the world,' Mark finished, resting against the table edge.

Old man Escott sat musing in the glow of the standard lamp.

'Yes,' he admitted finally, 'it probably will sweep the world, always providing you don't fall into one or other of the

15

pitfalls ahead of you. You don't suppose big business will let you have an easy time, do you? You don't suppose you will have a licence readily granted, do you — ?'

'Licence?' Mark interrupted. 'What licence?'

'The Government will demand one, be sure of that. Even radio transmission and reception in the ordinary way cannot operate without licence, so it is certain your system won't. Since no such departure exists in law special legislation will have to be brought in.'

'Fair enough. I'll see I get it.'

'And you propose starting a company, purely for the handling of freight?'

'Frieght to begin with, yes. Later, it will be people. And after that — Well, there's no limit to distance if the power is increased. I might even reach out into space.'

'In which case somebody will have to go into space ahead with a receiver. Had you thought of that?'

'Not very clearly. It's only a nebulous idea at the moment.'

'Don't start running before you can walk, Mark,' Escott warned, jabbing his pipe towards him. 'Stick to freight for a few years and then advance with extreme caution. Believe me, like all pioneers, you're going to be up against the devil of a lot of opposition.'

'I'm ready for it. I don't care who I stamp on or what I do, but I'm going to establish the Rowland Electronic Transmission Company as one of the most powerful organizations ever known. Claire's coming into it with a bit of capital, and so is my scientific partner Ted Shepley. I got the idea you and Mrs. Escott might be interested, too.'

'We'll be interested all right, Mark — when you get Government licence. Since the whole scheme is contingent on that it would be silly to form a company properly until you know you have permission to operate it.'

'I shall apply for it, of course.' Mark responded, thinking, 'but if a lot of haggling and procrastination blows up I'll override the lot of them and launch out anyway. Sometimes it is necessary in order to bring a slow-moving officialdom to its senses.'

'Do that and you'll lose the lot. The Government is stronger than you are, my boy.'

'Perhaps.'

Escott lighted his pipe. 'What do you mean by 'perhaps'?'

'I mean,' Mark answered slowly, clenching his bony hands, 'that I have discovered a terrific power. I own and control it and it is patented. I mean that I will not accept defeat from any source whatever. If I have to demonstrate to make myself understood, I'll transport a famous landmark to somewhere else — say Nelson's Column to the Sahara Desert. Whatever happens I am determined to establish myself, whoever or whatever gets in the way.'

'Not on my money,' Escott smiled, though there was an odd light in his eyes. 'I'll join in any legal enterprise which has great possibilities — such as this has — but I will not be a party to any deliberate flouting of authority. Claire, of course, is at an age to please herself.'

Claire did not speak. Mark wheeled on her. 'Anything the matter?' he asked sharply.

'Why no, Mark. Nothing. I'm still with you, no matter what you do.'

'That's good hearing, anyway.' Mark looked again at Escott. 'Maybe your way and the modern way are different, sir. In these days, if you are to get anywhere, you must override every obstacle of law and authority and prove you are the one who counts. Waiting for authority can drive you into the grave.'

'Maybe, but it's better to die an honest man than climb to the heights over everybody and everything.'

Mark straightened up. 'All right. I'll see what I can do about that licence and then let you know . . . Same time and place tomorrow. Claire?'

'Of course,' she smiled, rising. 'I'll walk with you to the end of the avenue.'

Mark nodded, said goodnight to Mr. and Mrs. Escott, and then departed with Claire ahead of him. When eventually she came back into the room, obviously thinking, her father gave her a serious glance.

'Claire, have you still enough faith in your father to take some advice?' he asked.

'Depends what it is, dad.'

'Giving it you straight from the shoulder it's this: cut Mark right out of your life. Make any excuse you like, but step out now.'

Claire smiled, not taking him seriously. 'You're — you're joking!'

'I was never more serious in my life. You won't see this business as I do because you're young and very much in love with that young man. Until now I've seen nothing wrong in him — just imagined him to be a good radio-television engineer with a tight pocket and a lot of unfulfilled ambitions. Now I know differently. He gave himself away tonight. He's absolutely corroding with ambition.'

'And what's wrong with that? Mark's only thirty, You wouldn't expect him to be anything else but ambitious, surely?'

'In a normal way, no — but he openly admits he is willing to tramp on everybody and everything to put himself right on top of the world. That wasn't just talk, either: he really means it. This discovery of his has lit a timber-pile and heaven knows where he'll stop.'

'But surely, dad, a step at a time and — '

'Step at a time!' Escott laughed scornfully. 'Why, right at the very beginning he talks of over-riding legislation. He can see only one thing, my dear — the elevation of Mark Rowland to a position of eminence and power, no matter what. He'll sacrifice everything to that end, including you if you are foolish enough to let him.'

Bewildered, Claire sank down to the settee and glanced at her mother. But Mrs. Escott did not say anything. Her husband's observations were the only ones that counted.

'In fact,' Escott concluded, lighting his pipe, 'I'm very much surprised at that young man — '

'But surely, dad, you can't deny that he has made a wonderful discovery?'

'I don't deny it for a moment. But it should be handled by men who don't

21

put personal ambition before normal progress. To be frank, Claire, I don't intend to put a cent into the company he's forming. I'd never feel safe — and no matter what he tells you, or how rosy a picture he paints, keep out. A man with insane ambition will do anything.'

Claire was silent, wondering vaguely what her father would say if he knew of the materials appropriated from the W.B.C. Mechanically she found herself answering.

'I can't step out now, dad. I'm too fond of Mark for that. However he behaves I'll stick by him.'

'I've no doubt of it, but will he stick by you?'

'I think he will,' Claire said, after a pause.

Her father made no comment this time, but his raised eyebrow was sufficient proof of his thoughts.

Meantime, Mark was on his way back to central London, a man lost in thought. But he had to emerge from it when, to his astonishment, he found his partner Ted Shepley waiting for him at his small flat.

'What in blazes brings you here, Ted?' Mark threw open the flat door and followed the stocky, snub-nosed scientist into the lounge.

'Trouble, of course. You don't suppose I'd break off my holiday in Brighton otherwise, do you?'

'Trouble?' Mark switched on the lights. 'What sort of trouble?'

'The law. Just after I'd 'phoned you about the safe arrival of that block of salt two plainclothes men turned up and wanted to know what I was up to.'

Mark's gray eyes hardened. 'What did you tell them?'

'I wriggled. I told 'em I was a radio ham experimenting, but since my license to do that doesn't cover the sort of apparatus I was using they didn't believe it.'

'Go on.'

Ted Shepley looked away. 'They had the apparatus taken away and warned me I'd receive a summons to appear in court. Near as I could make out they've got the idea I'm an enemy agent sending information or something. Can't blame 'em with so much Asiatic trouble brewing.'

'And that's the best you can say?' Mark asked deliberately.

'You want the facts, don't you?'

'Facts, yes, but I don't want a lot of defeatist excuses. You actually let them take away that equipment? Don't you realize how valuable it is, what they might find out for themselves? Dammit, man, can't you see that you've thrown all our plans into the ragbag?'

'I couldn't do anything against them, Mark!'

Mark lighted a cigarette irritably and paced around for a while, smoke pluming from his nostrils. Finally he seemed to arrive at a decision.

'Sorry I blew up,' he apologized. 'I suppose you couldn't do much else but give in — '

'And that isn't all. They wanted to know what I was doing pirating power from one of the main feed cables. As you know one of them goes right over that office block where I had the apparatus and it seems the load of juice consumed set the powerhouse authorities wondering. They put the police onto it, and so they came snooping.'

'Evidently it wasn't a good idea to peg onto the public power line,' Mark commented dryly. 'No other way to get the juice we needed, though, since we can't afford special generators.' He seethed for a moment. 'Money, money! Always that damned drawback to everything. With unlimited capital we could really get somewhere . . . Well, obviously we face a court case and we'll scramble through it as best we can — but in some ways it may prove a mixed blessing. The amount of advertisement we'll get will be worth it. Believe me I'll say plenty when called upon to explain. The thought of those p.c. men having taken away the apparatus worried me for a moment — but they can't do anything whilst I have a patent. Yes, thinking it over, maybe it's all for the best.'

'I hope so,' Ted muttered, helping himself to a drink. 'Getting away from our troubles for a moment, what is your next move? We've proved we can dispatch inorganic objects. Do we try and cash in on that or develop the next stage?'

'We cash in on what we've got because

we need money. I meant it when I spoke of the Rowland Company. I think I can get Claire Escott to join us too. Her capital won't be large but she'll make a useful bait for her old man who's by no means short.' Mark's gaunt face clouded. 'Trouble is, he wants to see the goods on the table in the form of a license, first.'

'I don't blame him. If we had thought of that earlier we wouldn't have got into this present mess.'

'Suppose you tell me how we could have convinced a lot of muscle-bound Government officials that we have a radio-transportation system? We couldn't have done it without recourse to photostats and demonstrations, all wasting our time and giving other engineers ideas. As things are we stand a far better chance of getting a license because some members of the public are bound to see the possibilities. Yes, I think we've won this round, Ted, not lost it.'

Ted did not answer, chiefly because he had not the confidence of Mark to turn an apparent defeat into resounding victory.

2

Atomic murder

The Rowland 'case' started in a mild way and then rapidly climbed to headlines — which was just what Mark wanted. The actual 'crime' of pirating power took second place to the amazing claim that solids could be sent by radio methods to any desired distance. Scientists mused on how this could be done; businessmen pricked up their ears; and the public in general crowded the courtroom as the case, starting in so small a way, assumed massive dimensions.

The outcome was that Mark Rowland was fined a comparatively negligible amount for the Brighton affair, and even this was paid for by a businessman — whom he had yet to meet. He emerged more as a hero than a villain, applauded by scientists and the general public alike for the discovery he had made.

Other smaller incidents followed in the train of the court case. The W.B.C., checking up on their stores of apparatus, accused Mark Rowland outright of theft, and then for some reason they mysteriously withdrew their charge and apologized instead. Claire Escott, in court each day with her father, lost her job through continued absence from it, and Escott himself, far from being convinced by the final verdict, only clung more rigidly than ever to his assertion that Mark Rowland was a man to avoid.

Not so Claire. She was with him at every opportunity and joined in his jubilation when the trial was over. For a reason that was not at first clear to Claire the celebration dinner was held in the Majestic Hotel where the prices were suited to millionaires.

'All very marvellous, of course,' she said, gazing around her, 'but we could have done with something much simpler. Mark. It's just throwing money away.'

'Just what I told him,' Ted Shepley put in, resplendent in a tuxedo.

'I never throw money away,' Mark

replied briefly. 'We are here at the request of Gordon J. Harper; who can be better called our fairy godfather. Gordon J., if you're not aware of it, is a multi-millionaire and his business is the transportation of freight to all parts of the world. He's taking the place of your father, Claire.'

Claire looked uncomfortable as Mark's grey eyes pinned her.

'I'm — I'm sorry about dad, Mark, but I can't make up his mind for him. He simply prefers to stay out.'

'As long as it doesn't affect you.'

'It won't. You know that. Surely I've proved it the way I've stayed by you?'

'Bless you, yes.' For an instant Mark relaxed and flung an affectionate arm about her shoulders; then he was the hard, ambitious scientist again as a resplendent maitre-d'hotel ushered an extremely fat and immaculate man through the velvet and gold wilderness.

'Here's Gordon J. now,' Mark murmured, rising. 'Remember, you two, whatever he says is right. With the money he's got he has to be.'

'Well, well, before me, eh?' Gordon J. had a high falsetto voice that did not match his bulk. 'Delighted — How are you, Miss Escott? Rowland — Shepley.' He shook hands in turn and then floundered into a chair. 'Well now, here we are, all secluded — and yet the nucleus of something colossal, eh?'

'I'm hoping so, Mr. Harper,' Mark smiled.

'Mmmm, yes. Time we had something to eat!'

A waiter appeared magically and the repast was brought; but it did not occupy the great Harper so much that he could not talk at the same time.

'We could have discussed this at my home, of course,' he said, blinking and grinning, 'but in that event it would have involved others being present. My wife, the servants, and so forth. You can't be private, even in your own home. In my office there's even less privacy. I don't trust anybody. I'm funny that way. And this is too important to go beyond us, eh?'

'Definitely,' Mark agreed politely, and with a grunt of agreement the big man went on eating. Then presently he drifted back to the point.

'I hope you realize, Mr. Rowland, just how much you owe to me?'

'You have already made known your generosity, sir,' Mark responded. 'You paid the cost of the trial and the fine — '

'I also silenced the W.B.C. when they looked likely for threatening you with that charge of theft. I couldn't persuade them to keep you on their staff — and indeed I did not try very hard since you obviously have other things to do from here on. I have also been successful, I learned tonight, in getting the government to grant legislation to permit your having a licence to operate your electronic transport system.'

'You've been remarkably kind, Mr. Harper,' Claire smiled.

'Kind? Me? No, I'm just a business man, Miss Escott. I see here a terrific possibility and I mean to develop it.'

'With my help, of course,' Mark observed dryly, and Harper gave a fleshy chuckle.

'Of course. What do you suppose I

know about scientific stuff? Not a dam' thing. What I am going to do is sink a sizeable capital in your company, which you mentioned during the trial. I will also undertake the purchase or erection of transmitting and receiving stations in various parts of the world. In return for all that I shall of course be the managing director of the company.'

'No,' Mark said flatly. 'That would give you too much power. The success of this whole project depends on my electronic system, remember, and if anybody is going to be managing director it's myself.'

'Of course,' Claire confirmed dutifully.

Gordon J. did not explode. He did not even stop smiling. Arguments were commonplace in his life, particularly in the matter of business.

'Without financial backing, how far will your project get?' he asked blandly.

'I'm quite prepared to start it in a small way,' Mark answered, but Harper shook his head.

'You wouldn't get anywhere, Rowland, and you know it. The moment you launch the big dogs are going to be after you

— the air, sea, and land transport companies. They've the hell of a lot of crushing power and they'd wipe you out. As an alternative you might sell your system to one of them and drop gracefully out of the scene. Without finance, and plenty of it, you're smashed before you start.'

Ted Shepley rubbed the end of his snub nose and took a drink. Mark sat with his lips compressed, his eyes hard.

'Apart from all this, if you are fool enough to try on your own, I must withdraw from my role as benefactor and ask that you make good the various sums I've had to spend on you. I don't want to do that, but business is business.'

Mark reflected. 'If the company were launched, with you as the managing director, where would I come in?'

Harper spread his plump hands. 'Naturally you'll all of you be in the company: you'll form it along with me. I simply wish to be in control so that I can make all the necessary arrangements to put the thing over in a big way — the only way in which it can succeed.'

Which started Mark arguing again — and it continued back and forth for over an hour; but in the end he was forced to realize that without unlimited finances he just could not move. Gordon J. achieved his object and sat fat and smiling.

'Everything will work out for the best, never fear,' he said. 'I can take care of the opposition very easily. Come to my office tomorrow and we'll make the whole thing legal with my solicitor. I've one or two boys who will also come in and bring us up to an honest seven.'

Breathing hard Harper floundered to his feet. He took his departure amiably enough, fixing ten the next morning as the hour of appointment. Mark watched him retrace his way through the soft lights and his lean jaw tightened.

'Have I got this whole thing wrong, or is he going to get more out of it than we are?' Ted Shepley asked anxiously.

'He may to begin with, but he won't in the long run. For the moment we've got to play the game his way because we've no money. Later on we — ' Mark checked himself and changed the subject. 'I'll see you home, Claire,' he said, holding her wrap for her.

'Which won't take long. I'm staying at the Albermarle Apartments.'

'You're what?' Mark frowned at her.

'Afraid it has to be that way, Mark, since dad and I ceased seeing eye to eye with each other over you.'

'Oh . . . Well, anyway, I appreciate your loyalty. Just let us get this company business sorted out and then we'll be married. Isn't there anything I can say to your father, which will make him change his attitude? If it's the licence that is worrying him, you heard Harper say he's fixing it.'

'Dad's right out of it,' Claire answered quietly.

Mark did not pursue the subject and, ten minutes later — having parted from Ted Shepley on the way — he took his leave of the girl. The following morning they all met again in Harper's office in the palatial Harper Building. Present besides Harper himself were three other men — lawyer Brooks, and two men connected with world freight.

The formalities were dispensed with as quickly as possible ending in a stock company capitalized at fifty million pounds, of which the lion's share was, of course, Harper's, who became managing director. Mark became technical director and Ted Shepley assistant director. Claire finished up as Mark's personal secretary, at his own request. The number of shares of stock and the valuation thereof had still to be worked out. All that signified for the moment was the legal registration of a company. Nothing could move until this was done.

'Fifty million may appear a large amount for a start,' Harper said, 'but we'll need every penny of it.'

'Compared to our own financial contributions you are the Lord of creation,' Ted Shepley commented, and then became silent as he caught Mark's grim look.

'When's that licence going to be through?' Harper asked Brooks.

'A week maybe. Parliament doesn't move fast. But you'll get it all right.'

'We'd better.'

'That doesn't stop us planning ahead,' Mark said. 'I want to get some action.'

'And you shall. Come into the next room: there's a world projection map there. We've got to get this thing worked out properly.'

The company moved into the next office and examined the enormous map occupying one wall.

'Naturally our main transmitter will be in London here,' Harper said. 'And we shall cover the world. Right, Rowland?'

Mark nodded. 'Nothing to stop it — but the further we go the more power we'll need. For the transmission of very heavy freight from London to Australia, the greatest earthly distance, we'll need transmitters able to handle ten million electron volts.'

'How big a building does that mean?'

'Have to work it out, but it'll certainly be a big one.'

'Whatever it is we'll get it,' Harper decided. 'Now as to routes. We shall need London-Australia, London-New York, and so forth. As well as receivers in the distant places we'll also need transmitters for the return transit of goods. Allow for that when working out your areas.'

'Something occurs to me,' the lawyer put in. 'Will this electronic transmission interfere with radio and television reception? If so we can look forward to trouble.'

'The interference will be negligible,' Mark answered. 'I can incorporate a screening system which will act much in the fashion of a suppressor.'

Now the method of transmission and reception was being discussed Mark became a little more cheerful, though it was plain from his expression that either something was lingering at the back of his mind — or he was trying to mature some kind of plan. He was working out, gradually, the safest way to be rid of Harper and take his place as the managing director of the ambitious little company. At the moment it was of course desirable that Harper, with his far reaching influence, should handle things — but, as usual, Mark was looking to the future.

The discussion of technical details and

locations for the transmission/reception stations, quickly abbreviated to 'T.R.' stations, took most of the morning, and during the afternoon Mark was present once more in Harper's office to discuss with the heads of electrical firms the equipment which would be needed. Things were certainly moving, but it was obvious many months would have to pass before the Electronic Transit Company — as Harper had insisted on re-naming it — could actually begin business. Meanwhile a vast scheme of canvassing went on behind the scenes.

In this development Mark had little interest, nor was his presence needed — so he utilized the time to marry Claire.

Her father was present to give her away at the almost regal ceremony — upon which Mark had insisted — but he said very little. So to the south of France for a honeymoon before commencing the hard routine of work which must eventually follow.

The required Government license was duly granted, covering a period of five years — then indeed there were rapid developments. In the heart of London an enormous square, but not very tall, building began to appear, the hoardings around it carrying the flamboyant announcement — SITE OF ELECTRONIC TRANSIT COMPANY. At the same time similar buildings were being erected in New York, Perth, Ottawa, San Francisco, Paris, and leading European and Eastern countries. In some cases permission had been hard to obtain but the influence of Harper had finally triumphed.

These were busy days for Mark and Ted Shepley. Together, Claire travelling with them as secretary and keeping track of voluminous notes, they flew about the world by fast 'plane, supervising the erection of the T.R. stations and the assembly of the equipment.

Eighteen months passed before they realized it, but it was two years before every T.R. station was in working order and the enormous network of 'transit lines' — completely invisible, certainly, but needing careful plotting — satisfactorily organized. When this happened, the newspapers carried front page splashes of the aims of the company. In a word, the business of transmission of inorganic objects by electronic process was ready to begin.

Mark had some two hundred chief electronic engineers working under him. They were scattered about the T.R. stations in various parts of the world. He, as the actual brains behind the whole project, occupied an extremely complicated 'brain-room' in the heart of the London headquarters, where he was in touch with the whole network of stations by radio-television and bewildering arrays of slavemeters showed him exactly what was going on in any of the T.R. stations so he could immediately rectify a fault if one arose. Into this 'brain-room' only Ted Shepley was allowed to enter. Even Claire and the great Harper were barred in case they disturbed Mark's concentration when he was on duty. When he was not, Ted Shepley took over.

Five firms rather timidly admitted that they were interested in the instantaneous-projection system and entrusted cargoes of steel, stone, and small machines to the

Electronic Transit Company. When their various goods arrived in Canada and New York respectively, unharmed, and only three seconds after the notified time of departure, they just couldn't believe it — but when they could their praise was resounding and from that moment onwards the success of the Company was assured.

At the end of a month the 'E.T.C.' was piled to the roof with freight, so Mark sent a demand to Harper for other subsidiary stations to be erected in various parts of Britain. Harper did not even demur since it was perfectly obvious that he had backed a winner.

'The only thing that worries me,' Ted Shepley remarked one evening, as he took over duty from Mark in the brain-room, 'is what we get out of all this. Business is booming in every direction and we haven't even chipped a saucer in our transmissions. But where does the financial rake-off go? We get good salaries, sure, as agreed — but it isn't what you wanted, is it?'

'Definitely not,' Mark answered, getting into his jacket.

'Then what's the answer? We don't just have to sit in here year in and year out, do we, sniffing at the profits we might have had?'

'I think,' Mark answered, 'you can safely leave me to handle the situation to the best advantage. We've only been going a month as yet and we'll need Harper when the air, sea, and land companies start bleating that we're taking their business away from them. In any event we shan't really start to coin the big money until we've discovered the way to transmit living bodies. I'm working on that now in between time . . . Well, see you tomorrow.'

Ted nodded and Mark took his departure. He strode down the corridor and looked in at the main office for Claire. As a rule they went home together, but to his surprise she was absent.

'Now what?' he muttered. 'Taking late letters from Harper. I suppose?'

He walked over to the private door and knocked. Harper's voice came from beyond.

'Come in.'

Mark did so and looked about him. 'Claire not here, Mr. Harper? Any idea where she's gone?'

'Yes — home,' Harper answered. 'And not in a very pleasant temper, either.'

Mark frowned. 'How d'you mean?'

'Let me tell you something, Mark, since you're evidently not able to see it for yourself. You're too damned secretive about everything. Your wife doesn't like it, and neither do I.'

'Secretive? About what?'

'That brain-room, as you call it. Do you and Ted Shepley belong to the company, or don't you? All information should be freely exchanged amongst the officials of the company, else how are we to get smooth working? Suppose something happened to both you and Shepley? What then? How would we carry on?'

Mark came forward slowly to the desk, his big mouth set.

'You wouldn't,' he answered. 'Which is just the way I mean it to be. If anything happens to me, or Ted, this company might as well shut down. I've taken care not to give any of the chief engineers the remotest inkling of the real heart of my transmission system. That's my insurance against accident.'

'What the devil do you mean?' Harper demanded bluntly.

'I mean that I don't trust you any more than you trust me. Nothing would suit you better than to have me, or Ted Shepley — or both of us — vanish from the scheme of things and leave you to run things. My wife you'd soon put in her place, of course. But you can't do it, Harper, not as long as you don't know how to repair a breakdown if one occurs.'

Harper gave a fleshy chuckle. 'Well, I can't say that I blame you making yourself safe, even if you are needlessly suspicious. All I want is amicable relations amongst every member of the company, and we're not getting it whilst you keep that brain-room to yourself. I think you'll find your wife, too, resents the idea of being shut out.'

'I have shut her out in case she lets something slip in conversation. That brain-room is strictly private, and it stays that way . . . In any case, even if I changed my decision and allowed you to see the room in action, you would not understand one scrap of it. You're no scientist.'

'That's nothing to do with it. As managing director I have the right to see what is going on, and your wife as your technical secretary and a stockholder, also has a right. Take the chip off your shoulder, Mark. All I want is a successful organization. I've no intention of getting rid of you — '

'I shouldn't think you would have, seeing I'm the brains of everything.' Mark appeared to be thinking swiftly. 'All right, come and have a look round. I don't need to tell you anything vital.'

Harper looked surprised at the sudden about-face, but he got to his feet readily enough and followed Mark's tall, ambling form down the corridor. The specially designed lock drew back as Mark released the combination and then he led the way into the maze of electrical equipment, Ted Shepley looking on in surprise.

'What's the idea, Mark?' he asked briefly. 'I thought you had made a rule that — '

'I can alter it, can't I?' Mark glanced at him briefly and then waved an ubiquitous hand. 'Well, here it all is, Mr. Harper. Study it for yourself.'

With genuine interest on his flabby face Harper began to prowl. Mark closed and locked the door, gave Ted Shepley a peculiar glance — which Ted could not interpret — and then moved up to the side of Harper.

'Here are the meters which show exactly how all other T.R. stations throughout the world are functioning,' Mark explained. 'Here are the clocks which show the different times, with the master-clock in the middle set to G.M.T. In this corner is the radio equipment by which we inform the appropriate T.R. station of what is coming and by which they reply. You will notice the T.V. screen also. That wall there is false, and has direct contact with the storage rooms, as you know. All freight is brought in here mechanically, so nobody else can enter, on an endless belt system. The belt ends just outside this room. Magnetic attractors, which you see there, move the

47

freight, however heavy, into the transmission area. There it is.'

Mark indicated a clear space in the center of the room. In the floor was a grid, and seven feet above it a massive horseshoe magnet and an array of tubes and attractor bars.

'In here,' Mark said, 'the original dissembly is carried out. The resultant atomic parcel is transmitted then to the main power room — which you know about already. They look after the task of 'broadcasting' the parcel to wherever it has to go. In here I merely watch the process on the meters and if they run into trouble I correct it for them. By that means I keep the actual secret to myself.'

'Yet transmissions are made from other countries,' Harper pointed out. 'Don't the engineers there know the secret?'

'No. They merely follow out orders without knowing the process involved. A man may drive a car perfectly, Mr. Harper, without having the vaguest idea what makes it go. Let me give you an example. Were you about to dispatch something when we came in, Ted?'

'I was looking through the dispatch notes for that consignment of agricultural equipment to Perth. There are two crates of them to go. Usually send them at this hour since it is a convenient day time in Australia.'

'Right — get them,' Mark instructed briefly, and though he still looked vaguely astonished at this decision to reveal everything to the eager-eyed Harper, Ted complied quickly enough. From the adjoining storeroom he wheeled two heavy cases, smothered in labels and manifests, and with the stamp of E.T.C. across them.

'Now, you observe?' Mark asked, as the cases were placed in the area of the magnet. 'They are dissembled here and then broadcast by the power department. Excuse me a moment — ' Mark turned aside to the intercom. 'Harry? Prepare to receive eight thousand electron volts load — for re-dispatch to Perth T.R. station. Notify them by usual radio beam.'

'Okay, Mr. Rowland. Standing by — Say, I thought you were off duty at this time?'

'Special demonstration,' Mark explained, somewhat cynically, and switching off he looked at the meters and then glanced towards Ted as he stood with his hand on the main power lever.

'Okay,' Ted said.

'Take a closer look, Mr. Harper,' Mark said, motioning. 'This dissembly process has to be seen to be believed.'

Harper nodded and came forward. Mark turned to one side to give him a clear view, and then Ted threw the switch. At the same instant as the generators hummed something else happened. Mark twirled around, gave a mighty shove, and sent the unprepared Harper stumbling hard against the already dematerializing crates.

Ted Shepley was so startled he forgot to switch off, and by then the thing was done. Harper dissolved into a mist along with the cages and the space was empty. Mark stood watching, only his taut features showing his mental reaction. Mechanically he turned to the intercom and switched on.

'Stand by to take load,' he ordered.

Then, 'Okay, here it comes — maximum surge.'

He switched off again and mopped his face briefly. Ted was staring at him fixedly.

'Mark — Mark, do you realize what you've done?' Ted came forward slowly. 'You've dispatched Harper to Perth, along with those cases. You've killed him!'

'Curiosity killed more things than a cat,' Mark retorted. 'Remember one thing. Ted: he met with an accident. Stepped too close and we couldn't do anything about it . . . I'm going to fix that angle this moment.'

Again he swung to the intercom: 'Hello! Mark Rowland here! There's been a tragedy, Harry. I had Mr. Harper in here taking a look around and now we can't find him. There's only one answer: he must have stepped into the dissembler area and got himself dissolved. His corpse will turn up in Perth. Advise them right away what's happened and tell them to contact me the instant reassembly is complete.'

'Right,' Harry agreed, with something like a gasp. Mark switched off, then his big mouth broke into a hard grin.

'Tough on our managing director,' he commented finally. 'We haven't got the transmission of living bodies worked out yet, so he certainly won't be alive. I hope.'

There was a scared look in Ted's eyes. 'Call it what you like, Mark, that was murder!'

'All right, so it was murder. And don't ever go saying it out loud, either, because you'd get it in the neck as much as I would. I'd drag you in with me, of course, since you were present when it happened. Just keep quiet and let me handle the situation — or better still, stick to the story of an accident. Curiosity on Harper's part.'

'But why did you do it, anyway? I thought Harper was a necessary evil?'

'He'd suddenly made up his mind, along with Claire, that he didn't like this room being sealed off. I knew that sooner or later he'd poke and pry on his own when I was absent, very soon silencing any opposition you might offer. So I took advantage of his curiosity and got rid of him.'

'And what happens now?'

'Since I'm the brains of this company I'll take over as managing director — which is as it should have been at first. We've got the capital we needed to get started and rid ourselves of Harper before he could rid himself of us — Yes. Rowland speaking.' Mark broke off, as the intercom buzzed.

'Direct radio from Perth T.R., Mr. Rowland. You're through.'

'Well?' Mark asked briefly, as the face of the man at the Perth T.R. station appeared on the telescreen. 'What sort of a load did you get?'

'Since we'd been warned what was coming it wasn't so startling as it would otherwise have been. We got the two cases all right — not a mark on them: and we also got the 'scrambled' body of a man.'

'Scrambled?'

'Yes. He's stone dead and almost unrecognizable. You say it's Harper, otherwise we wouldn't have known. We've had a surgeon examine him and it appears his internal organs are all in the wrong places and only his backbone is in one piece. The rest of him is a sort of . . . jelly. Shows one thing, anyway, we're by no means ready yet for transmission of living beings.'

'I'll report the facts to the authorities,' Mark said, adding a somber touch to his voice. 'Pity it happened that way. Harper shouldn't have gone too close. Put his corpse in a coffin and return it to London for burial. Okay.'

He cut the communication and then glanced at Ted, who was still looking dubious.

'If anybody looks into this business thoroughly there'll be the load of 'a lot of trouble,' he said. 'Harper was a mighty important man. You mightn't even be able to hold the company together now he's gone.'

'It wasn't Harper holding the company together,' Mark replied. 'It was, and is, our financial success. We'll go right on progressing. You see . . . And remember what I told you. One word out of season and it's the finish for both of us. Now it's time I went home.'

Ted nodded but he did not say

anything. As yet he had not had the time to assimilate things. Mark took his departure, his face still grim as he reflected on the almost involuntary manner in which he had rid himself of the man he hated most; but he took good care to change his expression to one of concern when he arrived home.

Claire greeted him coolly as he came into the lounge.

'You're late,' she said. 'I've had a meal set out for the last hour.'

'Had you waited for me, as you usually do, there would have been no need for that.'

'I had no idea how long you were going to be, and as I'd one or two things to do this evening I came on ahead. You don't object to that, surely?'

'If it were the real reason I wouldn't object at all,' Mark replied, moving to the end of the settee and looking down on her. 'Only that's not the truth. You left in a huff. Harper told me as much. Apparently you don't care for the secrecy of the 'brain-room'.'

'No.' Claire's look was quite frank. 'I

don't. I'm not only your secretary and a stockholder, Mark; I'm also your wife. I'm entitled to know what is going on, surely?'

'Harper thought the same thing. He insisted on seeing in the room tonight. Because of that he wandered into the danger area of the dissembly unit and before Ted or I could do a thing he'd been reduced to atomic aggregates. He turned up in Australia along with a consignment, stone dead and his body structure smashed to bits.'

Claire rose to her feet in horror, her eyes ranging Mark's ugly, sombre features.

'But how in the world did it ever happen?' she exclaimed.

Mark shrugged. 'He must have got too curious. That was one reason why I kept that room private. Too dangerous for those without experience. Had you wandered in the same thing might have happened to you. That's why I kept you out. As things are we have no managing director for the moment, though it's a foregone conclusion whom it will be.'

'There's likely to be a lot of rumours flying about,' Claire commented, thinking.

'I'm expecting that. Fortunately Ted was there too and saw what happened. After the initial commotion everything will settle down nicely, don't you worry. Certainly the company won't stop business. It's doing too well. I've told Australia to send Harper's body back for burial. There'll be an inquest, I suppose, in Australia first since that was where the body turned up.'

Claire nodded absently and at that Mark left her and hurried upstairs to freshen up. Afterwards he came down to his meal, but since Claire had already had hers she did not join him. She was still in the lounge when he presently returned in there.

'I'm going into the den to work on organic transmission,' he said briefly. 'Call me at suppertime.'

He had reached the door when Claire spoke. 'I suppose it would break your heart, Mark, to abandon work for once? Or does it occur to you that we have never had a moment to breathe ever since we returned from our honeymoon?

'There's no time to breathe, Claire, when we've a vast organization to build up. We've got to keep pushing on and on — or at least I have. Especially so now we've lost the influence of Harper. Just transporting freight about the world is nothing: it's a completely mastered problem. I've got to move people and livestock next and so improve our chances and our finances.'

With that he closed the door and left Claire with her lips compressed. She was beginning to feel like part of the furniture — and particularly an article to be sat on.

3

Across space

In the ensuing two weeks the E.T.C. came into the limelight once again and all the facts — except the true ones — concerning the death of multi-millionaire Harper were paraded. But there was no suggestion of foul play even though Ted Shepley was prompted now and again by conscience to say a good deal. He only kept his mouth shut because he feared for his own safety.

Australian law pronounced Harper's death due to misadventure and British law upheld that verdict. After this followed internal upheavals in the company itself. Just as Mark had foreseen, however, it was the mounting success of the company which kept it in being and he succeeded in over-riding, by majority vote, all opposition to becoming managing director. Financially, the company was undisturbed, though it would certainly not get any more from the executors of Harper who had their doubts, even yet, as to how he had really met his death.

Not that the finances bothered Mark unduly. He knew, as did the rest of the stockholders, that the E.T.C. could not fail to prosper, for it already had more transport orders than it could fulfil. Far from collapsing, it was necessary to enlarge the scope — and so in the succeeding months, when the controversy over Harper's death had abated, the E.T.C. spread its ramifications in all directions, both in England and abroad, and as it spread the freight receipts for the air, land, and sea lines correspondingly dropped. Things had reached the state where it was old fashioned to send goods by any other way but E.T.C. A great monopoly was growing.

At this stage, a year after its inception, Mark changed his title to 'Controller' and handed over to Ted Shepley the job of chief technical engineer — and it was in his capacity as Controller that Mark met and weathered the storm from his rivals.

The big shipping companies were the first to protest, and many of them sought through legal means to have the E.T.C. suspended from operation on the grounds that its methods were basically unsafe and that valuable cargoes and consignments might be lost. The law thought otherwise and so the E.T.C. remained untouched.

There was not much trouble from the airlines for the simple reason that they could not handle extremely heavy freight in bulk as could E.T.C.; but the storm from the land freight companies was violent indeed.

James Bronson, representing the Executive of the Amalgamated Land Carrier and Removal Services, spent over an hour one morning trying to talk Mark into a compromise. Partnership with the land carriers, perhaps, or perhaps an agreed figure to buy him out? To which Mark only smiled; then his big mouth set adamantly.

'You are wasting your time, Mr. Bronson. Far from going into partnership, or being bought out, the E.T.C. will shortly open a new service — that of transport for human beings.'

'Impossible!' Bronson declared, startled.

'It wasn't impossible for the cat's whisker radio to grow into television and radar, was it? To grow into the dissembly transport system of today? It's not impossible, believe me, as you and the rest of the world will very soon find out. In fact the best thing you can do is forget all about the old-fashioned means of transport for both goods and people and transfer your affections to us. We could do with your capital you could doubtless do with the dividends.'

This was sufficient to send James Bronson packing and from that point on no further efforts were made to stop the E.T.C. It was generally recognized by the air, sea, and land companies that their heyday was over and, behind the scenes, some of the biggest men made secret moves to clamber on the E.T.C.'s bandwagon.

All this helped to promote the growth and power of the organization. In two years it had cornered practically all the freightage business of the world, only failing where a die-hard conservative firm refused to trust its wares to 'new fangled' nonsense. There was hardly a town or city in the world that had not a T.R. station and the wealth of the concern was staggering now so many far-sighted business men had thrown in their lot with it.

So far, Mark was supremely satisfied, and he was a good Controller. But back of his mind ambition was still pushing at him. Claire could sense it and, in those rare moments when he did notice her presence, he made his feelings clear.

'We've got to do much better than this, Claire,' he told her one evening, almost two years after the company had started. 'We've reached saturation point in one particular development, and when that's happened it's time to make a move.'

They were walking together through the quiet summer evening towards home. It was too warm to use the car and, for once, Claire had had her way to get her husband to herself.

'Well, we can't just stop at transporting human beings,' Mark added at length.

'I've worked out how to do that, but it isn't the end of the road.'

'Then it ought to be.'

'Why should it? Science demands constant progress . . . '

'Maybe it does, but there are other things as well. You have wealth and tremendous power, and will accrue even more when you start the transportation of human beings, so why can't you stop there and remember that I'm your wife and would like a little attention now and again?'

Mark glanced at her in surprise. 'Well of course you're my wife. Since when have I neglected to observe that fact?'

'Since the day you married me,' Claire sighed. 'Apart from the honeymoon I've been only a secretary and a brick wall against which you throw your ideas and catch them on the rebound. I'm not so much interested in our fine house and loads of money, Mark. There are lots of vital pieces missing . . . A family, for one thing.'

'We can't be bothered with kids,' Mark said roughly.

'Or do you mean you can't?'

Mark came to a stop. 'Look, Claire, the sooner you see the vision beautiful ahead, the better! I'm not just stopping at this circumscribed world of ours with my invention. I'm going to reach out into space! The moon, Mars, Venus — even Pluto. Perhaps further than that. I feel that my dissembly system is the answer to space travel, except that we don't need a space ship.'

For a moment or so Claire forgot mundane things and was caught by his burning enthusiasm. Wherever science was concerned he could usually carry another along with him.

'Space travel? Other worlds? But how do you mean?'

Mark gripped her arm eagerly. 'It's obvious that if I can reach any point on the Earth I can also reach any point in space, simply by using more power. The only problem standing in the way at the moment is how to resolve an object on another world without a receiver — so, amongst other things, I'm working on an improved version of my system. I haven't got the answer yet, but I shall — and when I do it will mean that a living being can be projected across the void to another planet.'

'And will that be of benefit?' Claire's voice hesitated.

'What a question! Claire, where is your mind most of the time? Have you no imagination at all?'

'It simply sounds to me as though other worlds are likely to be up in arms at your sudden arrival — the populations I mean, if any.'

'None of the other worlds are populated, and to visit them without using expensive and unreliable rocket-driven spacecraft would be the biggest stride ever in scientific progress. However, that's in the future. The fact remains, the possibilities of my discovery are endless. There just isn't the time to bother with ordinary things; not as far as I'm concerned. I thought you realized the way things would be when you married me.'

'I just didn't think ambition would drive you so far, that's all. Don't over-reach yourself, Mark!'

He laughed shortly. 'With all the universe to work in? Hardly!

He said little more, and neither did Claire, until they had had the evening meal at home; then when they were in the lounge he asked a question.

'Would you care to see a demonstration of transportation of a living being?'

'When?' Claire asked, surprised.

'Tonight. I've arranged it with Ted. He's on duty at the main London station tonight and at exactly nine-thirty I'm going to transfer myself to his side. Just to show it can be done, and that I'm not afraid to do it as the pioneer. You might even care to come with me and break the monotony which seems to be obsessing you.'

'But — but when did you find out that it is actually possible to do this?'

'Quite a while ago. White mice, rabbits, and a dog have all been sent unharmed from here to Australia, the longest possible distance. They've not shown any ill-effects since, so there is no reason why it shouldn't be in order for a human being to try.'

'And you never said a word about the experiments!'

'Too busy thinking out their details, I suppose.'

There was anger in Claire's hazel eyes for a moment. 'That's the sort of thing I object to, Mark! You never take me into your confidence! You suddenly spring a thing and then get annoyed if I don't grasp the whole thing instantly.'

He grinned a little. 'Sorry. I didn't think it worth explaining as I went along. Anyhow I can tell you briefly where the human being system differs from the inorganic. It is necessary, obviously, to retain life in the person or living creature that is dissembled. That was what had me stopped for a long time, then I recalled a fact admitted by scientists of recent years — namely, that the body is actually objectified thought, a baser form of thought 'crystallized', if you will, into the formation of matter. That being so, the governing mind of a body would not be destroyed when the body was dissembled and afterwards rebuilt: it would simply mean that the mind inherent in it would go exactly where the body formation went, whether in its complete form or its atomic form. Just as a mind goes with a body even if the body is under anaesthetic. Whilst the body was in that state you could move it to the other side of the world and when it awakened the mind would be there just the same. See?'

'I'll take your word for it,' Claire said.

'Well, that's how it's done. The mind never leaves the formation of a body until actual death, at which the life-force fades out and separation is complete leaving only the mindless clay. The transition by my machine can be little different to going under anaesthetic — so if you want to come and watch, or perhaps try?'

Claire hesitated and Mark's piercing eyes studied her.

'Up to you,' he said briefly. 'Don't ever say after this that I don't give you a chance to share my secrets.'

That was enough to get Claire to her feet and he opened the door for her, ambling after her into the great experimental laboratory that he now maintained as an annex to his extensive home. It was similar to other dissembly units which she had seen except for the fact that it had double-magnets and the floor grid was unusually large and heavily earthed. Doubtless the magnetic devices were also very different, but into these she did not inquire.

'Nine twenty-five,' Mark commented, glancing at the electric clock. 'Time to get things warmed up and then tell Ted I'm coming.'

He switched on the generators, listened to them for a moment, and then turned to the television equipment. After a second or two Ted's face appeared on the screen.

'All set?' Mark asked calmly.

'Okay, Mark, when you are. I'm on six thousand e-volts, ample for one human being of your size.'

'Right. At exactly nine-thirty I — '

'Wait a minute, Mark.' Claire interrupted. 'I've made up my mind. I'll come with you. I suppose you have to know because of the 'load', or whatever it is?'

He gave a grave smile. 'Good girl. Claire's coming with me,' he added. 'This is one secret she's decided to share.

70

Better step up twelve thousand e-volts and be on the safe side.'

'Twelve thousand it is and best of luck.'

Ted switched off and Mark did likewise. Then he led the girl into the centre of the area under the magnets and she looked about her apprehensively.

'Mark, even if this succeeds with us you'll never make a paying proposition out of it. People will be scared stiff to trust themselves to this kind of gadgetry.'

'People were afraid of the airlines at first, yet look at them now! You can be a great help, m'dear, later on by telling the world your own sensations. Folks will accept it from an ordinary, everyday woman like you, instead of from a scientist like me. Now — ten seconds to go. Are you ready?'

'Uh-huh,' Claire whispered, and Mark could feel her quivering as his lean arm tightened about her shoulders.

Then it came. There was a faint click from the apparatus and at that moment it seemed to Claire that a total blackness descended on her. It was not unconsciousness, but a sense of utter immobility. She wanted both to cry and move, but she could not do either. In no possible way could she give expression to the fears that now beset her, and she could no longer feel the comforting grip of Mark's arm about her. She was dreadfully, terrifyingly alone in the utter dark. It seemed cold too: there was even a suggestion of icy wind blowing from somewhere.

Then it all dissolved into warmth and light returned. She was standing exactly as she had been, Mark's arm still about her shoulder. The only difference lay in the surroundings and the fact that Ted Shepley was watching intently. He came forward with a relieved grin and held out his hand.

'Made it,' Mark stated calmly, ushering Claire forward. 'Not that there was ever the slightest doubt but what we would.'

'All very well for you,' Claire told him, sinking onto a chair and breathing hard. 'My knees feel as though they're on ball-bearings. I've never been so scared in my life.'

'But, m'dear, we did it — and without harm,' Mark insisted. 'That's the point!

Good work, Ted. You handled the reception beautifully. This means,' Mark said, pacing thoughtfully about the huge 'brain-room', 'that we have come to another milestone in the advance of E.T.C. Tomorrow we start the publicity machine to work announcing our latest development — human beings anywhere at the speed of light. And up and up go our finances! I take it, Ted, that all the engineers who matter have been instructed in the slightly different technique essential for organic transport?'

'Yes. We're all set to go.'

'Good!' Mark rubbed his hands. 'I was just saying to Claire tonight, Ted, that the company is only at the very start of its power and glory. We've got the whole universe to work in.'

'Oh?' Ted took a seat and look surprised.

'Of course, man!' Mark confronted him. 'You don't suppose this miserable little planet is the limit, do you? Now we have organic transport worked out there's nothing further we can do on Earth here. We've got to extend — and that means into space. I'm working out the details of travelling to the moon. That will really be something.'

'Depends. Getting to a dead hulk like that won't do much good.'

'How do you know? Might be gold there: might be anything. Anyway, we're going to see, sooner or later.'

'If you say so,' Ted acknowledged; then he glanced around quickly as he saw Claire inspecting the complicated apparatus. He jumped to his feet, 'Better keep beside us, Claire!' he warned. 'This place is full of high voltages.'

'As Mr. Harper found out,' she commented. 'Was it here where he met his death? But of course it was,' she went on, answering her own question. 'This is the original 'brain-room' considerably extended isn't it?'

'Right.' Ted agreed, with a brief glance at Mark.

Claire strolled back, studying the area below the magnets where she and Mark had materialized. A puzzled little frown crossed her forehead.

'This is the reception and transmission

area.' she said, 'and presumably it was in this area that Mr. Harper met his fate. I can't quite see how . . . '

'What do you mean?' Mark asked, his voice brittle.

'Well, what on earth possessed him to walk into an obvious danger area like this? He was not a fool by any means, and he must have known that — '

Claire stopped. In glancing up unexpectedly she had caught the look on Mark's face before he had a chance to relax.

'I think it's time we were getting back home,' he said, forcing a grin. 'We've a lot of publicity work to do tomorrow . . . Ready, Claire?'

Her hazel eyes were regarding him absently, as if she were struggling to analyze something. Then she gave a little start.

'Ready? Yes, of course I'm ready. Good night, Ted: see you again sometime.'

'You bet,' he assented.

Mark, his face now expressionless, held the door open, and then followed Claire down the main corridor. In the hall he summoned the night porter and ordered him to get one of the staff cars. Whilst they waited Claire still mused to herself and now and again Mark shot a glance at her.

Her thoughts seemed to crystallize when they were being driven home, for she asked a question, in a voice quite unlike her own:

'It was murder, Mark, wasn't it?'

'Murder? Who?' He looked at her vaguely and then towards the partition which sealed them off from the car's driver. 'What the devil are you talking about?'

'You know perfectly well what I mean. Maybe the rest of the journey home will give you time to think up excuses.'

Mark folded his arms and smiled bitterly, turning his attention to the view of the night-ridden city through the windows. He said no more until they reached home. Then he poured drinks, handing one to Claire as she gazed at him searchingly.

'For God's sake, woman, stop looking at me!' Mark snapped. 'Here, take your drink. You need it after that transportation trip.'

'I got over that fairly quickly, Mark — but I need the drink just the same. It's a shock to realize I'm married to a murderer.'

Deep, consuming anger swept over Mark's ugly face for a moment and it twisted his big mouth. For an instant Claire felt sure he was going to strike her but instead he controlled himself and took a sip from his glass.

'You're getting very fanciful, m'dear, aren't you?'

'No. I wish I were — '

'You can't prove anything,' he interrupted curtly.

'Then you admit it's true?'

Mark hesitated, looking away. 'Yes, it's true. But nobody can prove anything, except Ted. And he daren't. I acted on impulse, and for the good of the organization as a whole. If Harper hadn't been wiped out we would have been, sooner or later.'

Claire was silent. She relaxed into the cushions, drinking slowly. Mark gave her a quick glance, wondering what exactly was going on in her mind.

'You did right,' she said finally, much to Mark's amazement. He lowered his glass, stared at the back of her blonde head, and then came hurrying round to the other end of the settee to sit beside her.

'You really believe I did?'

'Understand one thing,' she said, her voice quiet. 'I am not condoning murder: the very thought of it makes me feel sick inside. But I do know that Harper would have smashed you and Ted, which would have included me, had you not acted as you did. And you could hardly do anything else but get completely rid of him. As a man you naturally thought of killing him.'

'This is a relief,' Mark whispered, and finished his drink. 'For a moment I thought you were going to run home to daddy.'

'I'd get no sympathy if I did. He as good as shut the door on me the day I married you. I don't know why you could not have told me the facts. Since Ted knows them, why couldn't I?'

'Ted couldn't help knowing them; and I could not be sure of your reactions. I'm wondering how you knew Harper was plotting against us.'

'Oh, certain men he had who came to see him, peculiar telephone calls he put through, plans he had made for the future in which your name, mine, and Ted's had been dropped from the stockholders' list. He was up to something. On that evening when you found I'd gone early I confronted him with what I knew and we had a pretty fierce battle. I could hardly stay after it, so I came on home. Had he not — er — died, I would have resigned. I could not have gone back.'

'He told me you were burned up because I wouldn't show you the brain-room.'

'That was true. I mentioned it in conversation, but it was the least part of it.'

Mark put his glass on one side and threw an arm about the girl's shoulders.

'This makes me feel good,' he murmured. 'Believe me, Claire. I'm no killer.

I may be ambitious but murder isn't in the cards. That was just one of those things — and it must have been right because we've done nothing but progress ever since. The one thing you have to remember is: not a word at any time, anywhere.'

'Not that it would signify anyhow. A wife can't testify against her husband — nor would I. Whatever happens I have to stop by you, Mark, because you're all I've got.'

'And that's the only reason?' he asked sharply.

'No. Rightly or wrongly I love you — and I also feel that you need me as a brake for your wilder moments. I've come to realize one thing, though, being beside you. In the organization we're in we can't live as ordinary people. We're amongst wolves where the only rule is, destroy or be destroyed.

'At last you've grasped it!' Mark exclaimed, laughing. 'The schoolgirl has at last become a woman — and is the wife of one of the most powerful men in the world!'

*　*　*

The following day Mark launched his publicity campaign for the transport of human beings and living creatures. The directors of the company were duly satisfied by Mark's own transference of himself from place to place and Claire's verification of the trip she made — which experience she described over world-television in the E.T.C. sponsored programme — and, one by one, they themselves tried the system and were quite enthusiastic.

Nevertheless, the public in general was extremely chary of trusting itself to dissolution, exactly as Claire had foreseen. There was no hesitation on the part of cattle merchants to transport cows, sheep, horses, dogs and so forth, but the human element still hung shyly behind. Until a lucky break came Mark's way just as he was wondering what new move to make.

It so happened that a wealthy Indian dying in Bombay needed Harley Street's finest surgeon, and so urgently that a 'plane could never make the trip in time. E.T.C. transferred the surgeon to Bombay in exactly two and half seconds. The Indian was saved and the surgeon loud in his eulogy of this scientific miracle. Businessmen reasoned that if a surgeon, flesh and blood like anybody else, could do it, so could they. And then the flood began. In a matter of weeks the great termini of the E.T.C., ready prepared in every big city, had a continuous stream of passengers waiting to pass under the giant magnets which would 'disseminate' them to their destinations anywhere in the world.

The new accomplishment was an unqualified success, and though it would obviously be the work of years before the system became commonplace it had nevertheless cast its inevitable shadow over the more 'antiquated' forms of transport, though even Mark himself admitted that there would always be thousands who would never use the E.T.C. system, even as many had never been coaxed to air travel.

The newspapers, three of them owned

by E.T.C. itself, were soon lavish in their eulogy of Mark Rowland's genius. He had made the world shrink, cut time to a minimum, speeded business and done away with much of the clumsy inconvenience of normal travel. He had not been successful in obliterating the much-vexed Customs, but his experts were working on it. He himself, leaving Claire most of the time to act in his stead as Controller, was busy in his laboratory perfecting further uses for his dissembly process. The moon was firmly fixed in his mind, and nothing would satisfy him but that he reached the satellite.

It took him considerable time to work out a possible method, chiefly because there were periods when he had to be present as the actual Controller of E.T.C. to solve matters that needed his personal attention. But, slowly, out of the infinity of notes and tests he made he finally produced what he believed was an exact and workable process — and, following his usual custom, he did not say a word until he was ready for a demonstration. This time he invited not only Claire and

Ted Shepley, but also the leading scientists of the day. There were no absentees in the big residence-lab on the night of the test: Mark's fame as a radio-television scientist was too compelling for that.

'This time, my friends, we get another variation in the system,' he announced, standing near his apparatus and surveying the many interested faces turned towards him. 'And of course it is unique, as may be claimed of anything developed by E.T.C.'

Claire winced a little to herself. Mark, the shameless egotist, was at it again.

'My main trouble,' Mark continued, 'has been to devise a method whereby an object may be resolved at the other end without recourse to a receiver, and now I think I have it. If equations don't lie — and they don't — I have the right answer. For obvious reasons I shall not explain every intricacy. Let me say that the 'resolving' is accomplished by reversal of the dissembly process before the object can reach its destination. Plainly this can only happen over long distances. On

Earth it could not be done because our furthest point is reached in a few seconds. To the moon, however, the distance is two hundred and forty thousand miles average, which at the speed of light is one and half seconds approximately for the actual journeying time. Taking into account the few seconds used at this end in the dissemination process we can say with certainty that from here to the moon would take about five clear seconds from dissolution to resolution.'

'Which is certainly moving some!' Ted Shepley commented, and some of the scientists laughed.

'Assuming five seconds as our time,' Mark continued, 'we reverse the dissolution carrier beam at the fifth second. That automatically operates like a receiver, in that the atoms formerly dissembled are now forced back into their original state, and materialization results. In other words the receiver goes with the object, but in the form of a projected controlling beam that, in its first stage is a dissembling vibration, and in its last stage a re-assembling vibration. That is as near as I can outline it. Obviously, the greater the distance the more easily the changeover can be handled. Mars, for instance, at forty million miles, would mean a time lag of about five minutes, giving us ample chance to operate.'

'And would this method carry human beings?' one of the scientists questioned — a cadaverous, grey-haired physicist by the name of Dean Baxter.

'No reason why not. I shall make sure with animals first, animals prepared, that is, to stand the lunar conditions.

'For the initial experiment tonight, however, I have made all the necessary arrangements for sending a large-sized bomb. The bomb contains a cocktail of fluorescent chemicals in with the explosive, so that the flash, if it resolves on the moon as it should, will be clearly visible to the astronomers who at this moment have their telescopes trained in readiness. The moon is at the half phase and I have worked out the necessary computations for the bomb to land on the night-half of the moon, which will render the flash all the more distinct. I have also arranged that Mount Wilson observatory, which has the best viewing conditions, shall televise the scene in their biggest reflector. Publicity, my friends! Always the most valuable asset of the E.T.C.! As for us, we have an unusually clear night, so we can view things for ourselves.'

Mark turned to the apparatus, switching on the radio.

'Okay, Harry, to take up the load from my private laboratory?' he asked.

'Everything's ready, Mr. Rowland. We're standing by to feed two million e-volts. Take everything we've got, with slave stations helping, but I think we can do it. Radio and television will blank for a moment under the surge.'

'Right. I'll give you the final signal presently.'

Mark turned to the dissembly area and, now they realized they were looking at a large-sized bomb standing in the centre of the magnetic plate, the company looked vaguely apprehensive. Up to now they had not regarded the conical-shaped object with the copper nose as anything dangerous.

'Are you quite sure that thing can be reduced to atomic aggregates without exploding?' Ted Shepley asked anxiously.

'Quite sure. I have already tried it on a very small scale. There is nothing to fear, and it cannot explode without its automatic fuse operating. That is timed for eight-ten, five seconds from — now!'

Mark threw in the main switch and then spoke sharply into the radio. 'Okay — all yours.'

The bomb faded from sight and Mark headed quickly through the laboratory's rear doorway into the grounds. Claire, Ted, and the remainder of the audience hurried after him. Outside it was mild but clear, the half moon sailing just below the zenith.

'Five seconds are up by now,' Ted remarked, craning his face upwards. 'I don't see anything yet — Anyway, did you reverse the beam? I didn't see you do it.'

'It's automatic,' Mark replied shortly. 'It has to be to permit of me going to the moon at a later date without having any assistance at the transmitting end — There she is!' he broke off, in a triumphant yell.

Everybody was too astonished to comment for a moment. But there was no doubt that on the dark area of the moon there momentarily appeared a brilliant spot of light, approaching the intensity of a first magnitude star. In the transient glare the moon looked as though it had reached its full phase — then the glare was gone and the half moon remained.

'We did it!' Mark cried, doing something like a war dance as he gripped hold of Claire. 'It works! A bomb resolved over space! 'Scuse me!' he broke off, and raced back into the laboratory to contact Mount Wilson.

In a few moments the chief of the observatory came through on the radio television. He was looking warmly excited.

'No doubt that you did it, Mr. Rowland!' he exclaimed. 'And our heartiest congratulations. We relayed it by television as you asked and the engineers report perfect reception. Everybody in the world, who was looking in must have seen it.'

'Good.' Mark breathed hard. 'Where did the bomb land?'

'It's not possible to say with accuracy

until the sun gets higher on the lunar surface. Near as we can tell you blew hell out of a lunar 'sea-bed'.'

'Keep me posted — and thanks.' Mark switched off and turned to those gathered around him. He spread his hands, to almost immediately find them seized and pumped up and down in congratulatory praise.

'A magnificent performance!' Dean Baxter enthused. 'This isn't just a radio accomplishment, Mr. Rowland. It is the conquest of space in a way nobody ever thought of before. No clumsy space machines with dangerous explosive fuels; no initial take-off drag. And no lingering weeks in the void. There at the speed of light!'

'Correct,' Mark agreed, smiling calmly. 'The next thing I do is work out how to send living bodies — and that should not be a big problem since I can already do it with Earth stations. For the moment the world can acknowledge that E.T.C, has done it again . . . And that calls for a celebration,' he broke off, his mood suddenly changing to gaiety. 'This way. My friends, to the champagne!'

4

Wealth of the void

Next morning Mark was back at work again. As usual he was consolidating his position and deriving immense satisfaction from the worldwide reports of his successful experiment. Claire too was pleased, though not very demonstrative. She could never feel sure of Mark; never guess where his boundless ambition would finish now he had the void itself to play around in.

'I've things to do,' he told her, when breakfast was over. 'Nothing very important at the office today — nothing you can't fix anyway. See that consignment for Multi-Metals goes through okay to Ceylon, won't you?'

'Surely — but what are you going to do?'

'Do? Find a way to send myself where the bomb went, of course! Once that's done we have space travel almost in our grasp for the community at large.'

'Almost? I should have thought journeying to the moon *is* space travel.'

'Not entirely. It's only a testing ground. Mars is the next stop, or Venus. A dead world is no use except for experiment. Well, be a good girl. I'll see you later.'

Actually it was towards nine that same evening when Claire saw Mark again. She found him in the laboratory, but her intention of reporting to him the day's activities vanished as she beheld him. He was lumbering about in a pressure suit, enormous gloves and boots on his hands and feet, the only thing missing being a helmet.

'About time you showed up,' he said. 'I've been waiting for you.'

'Sorry I couldn't come sooner. There was a mix-up on the Continental Transit and I had to sort it out. What in the world are you dressed up like that for?'

'This is a spacesuit, which I thought should have been obvious to you. Helmet's over there. I had it made long ago in readiness for my experiment.'

Mark hesitated, clearly steeling himself to the next words. 'I've decided to make a leap to the moon, tonight — to the sunward side.'

'What! So soon? But I expected weeks of experiment.'

'So did I, until I discovered that sending a living body is identically the same method as sending one on Earth here. To test it out I sent a donkey to the moon early this evening just after moonrise and had Mount Wilson report on it. Their reflector is powerful enough to pick up an object the size of a donkey — or a man — and they reported it landed in one piece, but dead of course. No air to sustain it. I couldn't send it in a spacesuit because I wouldn't have known if it was inside it.'

'But you haven't proved one can cross such a gulf and live, Mark! It's too risky!'

'I'll live all right.' He gave his sardonic grin. 'If I don't, everything is willed to you so why should you worry?'

Claire flushed. 'That's a pretty beastly thing to say, isn't it?'

'Sorry.' Mark turned away for a

moment; then looking back at her he said, 'Where human life is involved it is essential for somebody to be at the transmitting end. Not like sending something inorganic. I can't afford the risk of not getting back ... I've set all the switches and all you need to do is follow directions to bring me back — '

'But do I have to do it now? I haven't freshened up or had a meal — '

'Those things can wait. The moon's position waits for no man, and Mount Wilson is all set. You've only just come in time as it is. Now look — to dissemble me you throw this switch. To bring me back you throw this one, and you are not to move the return switch until exactly thirty minutes have passed, thirty minutes from my final dissolution before your eyes. Understand?'

'Yes,' Claire assented quietly.

'I hope you do, otherwise it's the finish for me. I am going in this spacesuit so I can survive the airless conditions when I materialize on the Moon. You won't be able to see if I get there, but Mount Wilson will be on the televisor there. I'm taking various instruments and tools so I can make tests of lunar possibilities. Right?'

'Right,' Claire agreed.

Mark was silent for a moment, studying her. She met his flinty gaze calmly.

'What a superb chance you have!' he said finally. 'If you forget to move that lever you can ditch me for good on the moon and not a person in the world would be able to do anything to you. They'd simply say you are inexperienced and I shouldn't have been such a damn fool. After thirty minutes my air supply will start giving out.'

'I'm sorry,' Claire said, 'that you don't think any more highly of me than that.'

'I'm not thinking of you so much; I'm thinking that you perhaps haven't forgotten I wiped out Harper.'

'We went over all that long ago, and I said I thought you justified. Even if I didn't you don't suppose I'd strand you on the moon for revenge, do you?'

'Just don't let me down, Claire, that's all,' Mark said quietly, genuine entreaty in his voice — then he kissed her rather coldly and proceeded to screw on his helmet. This done he switched on the audiophone of his spacesuit and spoke into the microphone.

'Okay, Mount Wilson. I'm on my way. My wife is in control from here on.'

'Best of luck,' responded the voice from the speaker, and at that Mark took up his position in the dissembly area, giving Claire a nod to commence operations.

She pulled down the main switch as she had been instructed and Mark tensed himself in readiness. Since it was not his first 'trip' by the electronic process he felt he was more or less prepared for what was coming. In a second or two he found how wrong he was. Blackness descended in the normal way, but it was followed by a ghastly reeling sensation as though he were in the midst of a falling dream from which he could not awaken. All the terrors of hell roared in on him in those five ghastly, anguishing seconds whilst his atomic aggregates were disseminated across 240,000 miles of space.

He felt convinced he must die, and it was at this second that the headlong drop ceased, automatically timed, and he discovered he was lying flat on his back, staring through his helmet-visor at brilliantly winking stars in a coal-black sky. Then heat began to reach him even through his insulated spacesuit.

He scrambled to his feet and immediately found the sixth-less gravity playing him tricks. He turned a somersault, staggered, and at last regained his balance; then he stood drinking in the astounding sight that his scientific skill had made possible.

He was on the daylit side of the moon, the torrid rays of the unmasked sun soaking him in searing heat. He gave one glance towards it, then jerked his eyes away. But his dazzled retina carried an impression of liquid fire, prominences girdling the edge of the luminary. He began moving, marvelling at the fact that the shadows were utterly black and marked out in frost, due to, the absence of air for diffraction of light and diffusion of warmth.

Apparently he had landed in a crater. Its walls were around him, though far distant. Javelins of hardned lava and pumice, some higher than Earthly cathedrals. And everywhere an utter airless desolation. Then, raising his head, he saw Earth between two distant peaks — a blue and friendly ball, crescented on the dayside. He thought of Claire beside the apparatus and still wondered if she would bring him home again — or had he treated her so badly that she would take this heaven sent chance to be rid of him for good?

'Up to her,' he growled to himself. 'Science can't stand still, not even for Claire.'

He began to prowl carefully, measuring himself against the light gravitation. As he went he removed instruments from his belts and watched their reactions. At the end of fifteen minutes, during which time he pictured the Mount Wilson giant reflector picking up his movements, he paused and whistled to himself.

'It's unbelievable!' he whispered. 'Uranium by the ton; gold; silver; pure carbon ores . . . Dammit, this place is worth untold millions!'

There was no doubt about it because the instruments could not lie. Below the surface of the moon, and not very far down either, there were countless elements of extreme value on Earth, and the more he realized it the more Mark smiled to himself — and went on prowling. Then other matters crowded in on his mind. His air supply was thinning a good deal and he was becoming dizzy. His watch said the thirty prescribed minutes were almost up. Would Claire bring him back, or not?

He sat down on a pumice rock to take the strain off his labouring heart. A glance around him assured him that he had not stepped out of the two-mile area encompassed by the beam that had brought him here. No, everything was all right, providing Claire . . .

Then he was in darkness, gulping for life, whirling endlessly in a falling dream, flying through the gulfs of eternal space, through a bottomless hole. Anguish and a thousand devils, the conviction of death battering into his consciousness, which faded with the realization he was on his back once again looking up at huge horseshoe magnets and feeling the hands of Claire dragging at his bloated arms and shoulders.

With an effort, and her help, he staggered up and sat down in a chair. She quickly unscrewed his helmet for him, ran into the house, then returned with brandy. He gulped it down, breathed hard, and then gave his crooked grin.

'Good girl,' he whispered. 'You did it!'

'What else did you expect?' she asked seriously. 'How do you feel? You look all in.'

Mark began, to recover slowly. 'It's a ghastly business, Claire. Falling dream without end — But hell, it was worth it! That area of the moon's crawling with wealth! Gold, silver, diamonds, uranium — Scattered around for the picking up, according to my instruments. I'm claiming that crater as my personal possession in law before I announce anything.'

'I watched you,' she said. 'Mount Wilson got you clearly in the reflector and televised it back to me. You were only a speck, but at least I could see you. It was uncanny, somehow.'

'I hear you're back all right, Mr. Rowland,' came the voice of Mount Wilson in the speaker, and Mark jumped.

'I left the apparatus on in case I needed to speak in a hurry,' Claire explained.

'Then you should be more careful,' he breathed angrily. 'Don't you realize they must have picked up all I just said?'

Claire looked startled for a moment, then Mark had brushed past her and seated himself before the radio equipment.

'Yes, I made the trip successfully. Where exactly was I located whilst on the moon?'

'Tycho crater, Mr. Rowland. You moved north-eastwards. If possible I'd be glad if we could have a detailed statement from you concerning the moon's characteristics.'

'Naturally. I'll arrange it as soon as I can. Thanks for your co-operation — but for the moment I don't want too much said about my activities.'

On the screen the observatory chief's face was surprised.

'Until I have every detail worked out,' Mark added. 'The moon is only a proving ground, after all. I'm going to reach further yet — to Mars, and even beyond that.'

With that he switched off and then got to his feet. He glanced at Claire and clenched his fist. 'If only that radio hadn't been in action!' he muttered. 'They *must* have heard me at Mount Wilson!'

Claire shrugged. 'Supposing they did? They're men of honour.'

'I doubt it!' Mark grinned cynically. 'No man has much honour when he hears of the discovery of incalculable wealth.'

'That's judging people by your own standards, Mark.'

'What other standard is there? I'm going to make myself safe by claiming the crater — legally. And not in the name of E.T.C. either. Whatever can be excavated from the crater belongs to me since I found the way to get to it.'

'And nobody else can get to it — short of building a spaceship at a cost of billions — unless you let them, with your apparatus,' Claire pointed out. 'Why get so excited about it? The wealth may be there, but nobody can touch it unless you say so.'

Mark relaxed a little. 'Yes . . . Yes, I suppose that's right. I'm getting excited for nothing, maybe. All the same I'm going to safeguard things first thing tomorrow.'

And he did; and since he possessed considerable influence in the affairs of the city a good deal of red tape was swept away so that his legal claim to the mineral rights in the crater could be made good in law. There was considerable controversy and opposition from other countries and the scientific community, but Mark's wealth and influence, backed by his high-powered legal team, eventually prevailed. In fact it established a new law entirely known as Interplanetary Claim Regulation.

The signed and sealed papers deposited with his bankers made Mark a little more comfortable, but not entirely. He would have wished that the newspapers had not been so loud in their publicity concerning his successful lunar trip. Though he said nothing about the moon's staggering wealth he did realize that it was now generally acknowledged that, through his apparatus, the moon could be reached, the vast majority of its surface still unexplored. And he also knew that quite a few ambitious spirits were probably even now plotting how to make capital out of the fact.

The directors of E.T.C. naturally wished to know what he intended doing next, but all he would say was that his interplanetary experiments had only just begun. When Mars had been reached, then, granting the planet was worth visiting, even if only for tourists, inter-planetary travel might begin.

To the Mount Wilson observatory, and indeed, all astronomical bodies, he supplied first-hand facts about the moon as he had discovered them, but never once mentioned the wealth he had detected. This done, and his affairs as Controller being almost up to date, he retired again for further experiments, this time using Mars as his objective.

As on the previous occasion a bomb was used and scientists were gathered together to watch the experiment. The bomb contained special chemicals, principally magnesium that would generate a brilliant flash — rather than sheer destructive force — since, over 40 million miles, the flash would not be easy to detect. However, his mathematics were again correct and, minutes after the dissolution of the bomb from his laboratory, Mount Wilson reported a point of light visible on Mars and quite undetectable to the naked eye.

Mark was satisfied. The next thing he must do was study Mars and as before he put Claire in charge of the apparatus and she dutifully followed every instruction. But it was a shaken, nearly hysterical Mark who returned from the red planet. He could not speak coherently and was obviously desperately ill. For several weeks medical science despaired of his life, then gradually he began to mend.

'There's a lot to be done, Claire,' he whispered, on the first day he became rational. 'The human body can't stand a vast distance. It tears you to pieces. I died a thousand deaths both ways on that

Martian trip. It was bad enough going to the moon, but over forty million miles — it's intolerable . . . '

Claire was silent. The big bedroom was shaded and Mark looked like a ghost as he lay in the bed.

'How are things?' he muttered. 'We're still progressing? Still making money?'

'Of course, Mark. We can't help but make it. Why don't you rest easy and let the company look after itself for awhile? I can take care of everything.'

'It's all I live for, Claire. I can't help but think about it.'

'What,' Claire asked presently, 'did you find on Mars?'

'Sand. And nothing else. I couldn't investigate far for fear of getting out of the beam area. But Mars seems to be desert and completely dead. Thin air, light gravity, and very cold. Not even any eroded civilizations for tourists to look at . . . Maybe I'll do better with Venus, though I doubt it, based on what we already know of that planet.'

'You're not going to attempt Venus, Mark, until you've found some way of neutralizing the disastrous effects of the journey.'

'Right,' he whispered. 'For once we're agreed . . . '

It was the driving urge to get back to his experiments, and also bring affairs up to date with E.T.C., which brought Mark back to health eight weeks after his return from Mars. It was generally known throughout the world that he had gone as far as Mars and back, and now he was 'in circulation' again it was also known that he did not intend to put space travel among E.T.C.'s amenities until he had proved it perfectly safe. Which, of course, shed quite a heroic light upon him.

Again he experimented, his attention far more absorbed by safe space-transition — as he insisted on calling it — than the operation of E.T.C. Claire he felt he could trust to be his deputy, so he threw all his recovered energy and undoubted scientific genius into evolving a new method of travel whereby the sickening effect could be neutralized. But, though week succeeded week, he failed to master the problem.

'It's infuriating,' he told Claire one evening, when she arrived home. 'I've worked out everything theoretically — stresses, strains, balance, vibration. I can even produce a complementary form of energy to stabilize the shifting of the electronic 'parcel', which is the cause of the disturbance, only I'm short of a strongly reactive element. No, not even that. I need a catalyst.'

'A catalyst? What's that?'

'That's hard to explain. A catalyst is an element that changes the character of another element — an unknown factor as it were. No scientist knows what a catalyst really is: it simply has the inherent quality of doing something. According to my calculations I can make the vibrations of copper do exactly what I want in the way of stabilization if only I can find a catalyst to alter the basic state of the copper. Without that I'm sunk.'

'Surely there must be one somewhere?' Claire asked.

'Not that I can find. I've tested every darned element in the Periodic Table, so I — '

Mark broke off in surprise as the

laboratory door suddenly flew open. Since he and Claire both knew it had been locked at her entrance it was an incredible thing to happen. Then it explained itself as a figure entered holding an automatic. Behind came four other figures — all men, all well dressed, all holding automatics.

'Dean Baxter!' Mark exclaimed blankly, recognizing the famous physicist. 'What the hell's the idea of bursting into my home and laboratory like this?'

'Sorry,' Baxter apologized cynically. 'If we'd have come in the ordinary way you might have become suspicious. We had to do it by surprise. We've taken care of the servants so you don't need to waste time in that direction.'

Mark's bewilderment was complete. He still could not assimilate the fact that five of the most important men in science had burst into his home like common gunmen.

'What do you want?' he asked deliberately.

'A trip to the moon,' Baxter answered. 'It's as easy as that. Don't say it can't be done because you've already proved that it can. As to the reason — Well, though we may all be scientists, my colleagues and I, we also have a natural love of wealth. None of us is particularly affluent — compared to you, that is. And certainly nobody has so much money that they cannot do with more. Since the moon is redundant with wealth we decided to form into a clique and — collect.'

'Who told you the moon is redundant with wealth?' Mark demanded, glaring.

'You did, my friend. Thank you very much — and Mount Wilson verified it. A pity we have to forego our high professional principles for filthy lucre, but there it is.'

'I told you?' Mark stared in amazement. 'When?'

Baxter was silent but his eyes strayed to Claire. Instantly Mark swung upon her. 'Out with it, Claire! What's he talking about?'

'They came to see you when you were ill,' she replied. 'Only natural, as brother scientists. You didn't recognize them, though, and raved about gold and diamonds and uranium on the moon — '

'That all?' Mark asked in contempt, looking at Baxter again. 'You ought to have more sense than heed the ravings of a man in delirium. The moon is just pumice rock.'

Baxter shook his bead. 'Mount Wilson has verified your statement about incalculable wealth, Rowland. After you made it, even though it was plain you were raving, I contacted Mount Wilson and asked them if the region in which you explored was known to contain valuable minerals and deposits. The reply was that they couldn't say, but that they had heard you remark, upon return, that you had discovered vast wealth.'

Mark was silent, his fists clenched. Baxter gave a grim smile.

'Wealth like that isn't just for one man, Rowland,' he said. 'It needs sharing — and amongst scientists. Hence our reason for being here.'

'You can't touch a single scrap of that wealth!' Mark snapped. 'I registered the mineral rights in that crater in my name the day after I returned from visiting it.'

'A scrap of paper with official signatures has little power when men are decided upon something,' Baxter replied. 'Wars through history prove that . . . Now stop talking and project us to the moon, and back! Don't be alarmed, man. We don't want all the wealth there is — only as much as we can carry back in gold and diamonds. We're not even interested in uranium because we haven't the necessary containers to safely transport it. Later, of course, we may develop new schemes.'

Mark still had a look of complete impotence on his lean face. He knew full well that this was only the beginning of trouble, that in time these scientists, as ambitious as himself, would fight him to the death for a claim on the moon's treasures.

'Hurry up, man, and get moving!' Baxter commanded.

'Very well,' Mark agreed, with surprising suddenness. 'I will get the necessary spacesuits. There are half a dozen as it happens, of various types for me to test the most useful type . . . '

'Half a dozen is just right,' Baxter said.

'Start counting again,' Mark suggested. 'There are only five of you.'

'I make it six, including your wife.'

Claire recoiled in alarm and Mark frowned. 'Where does my wife fit into it?'

'Let's call her our good luck mascot,' Baxter suggested.

'You don't think, we'd be fools enough to let you project us to the moon, do you, without a guarantee of our return? We know enough of your system, from your own explanation, to realize that the one beam includes everybody — so any funny tricks with that will also include your wife.'

'I won't go!' Claire cried huskily. 'Mark, I won't make that awful journey!'

'If you don't you can see your husband shot down right here,' Baxter flashed at her.

Claire hesitated and Mark gripped her arm. 'We can't answer back,' he said. 'And I'm not risking being shot at this stage in my experiments, either. I'd go myself in your place and let you run the controls, only six people take a lot of handling.'

'And you'll stay right here and handle it,' Baxter ordered. 'We'll see to that. Now get those spacesuits!'

Mark did as he was told and threw all but one suit on the floor. The sixth one he held for Claire and she began to get into it slowly.

'You won't find it so terrible,' he murmured. 'We may not see eye to eye in some things, m'dear, but in a crisis we do stand by each other. I'll bring you back safely, and these claim-jumpers with you. By that time I'll have worked out how to finish them off, I hope.'

Claire would probably have protested even further but he did not give her the chance. He screwed her helmet in place and then looked at the five men. Baxter switched on his audiophone.

'You've got a couple of fire-axes on the wall there, Rowland; we'll take them. And a belt of detector instruments, if you please.'

Since the physicist still held a gun in his big hand Mark complied with instructions. Indeed each man, and Claire also, was fitted out with the necessary instruments and tools for small-scale mining — and, ever wary, Baxter insisted on five minutes delay in starting whilst he tested his own suit, and that of his colleagues, to be certain there were no faults in them. Claire he did not bother with, satisfied in his own mind that her husband would not deliberately sacrifice her.

In the interval of testing Mark contacted the major power rooms and the necessary computations. He thought once of saying that the moon was in the wrong position, then knowing Baxter was too smart to be fooled by that, he changed his mind. So, finally, the six were standing under the dissembly plate and Mark threw the switch. They faded from sight, and his eyes remained on the clock. Mount Wilson he did not contact for the simple reason he had no wish to reveal how completely he had been caught out by his rivals.

For the six who had been projected into space there followed a similar terrifying experience to that endured by Mark himself, a strain so tremendous that, by the time materialization on the moon was complete, it left Claire almost prostrate. The men moved her to a position just out of the blinding glare of the almost vertical sun and then began their explorations. As Baxter had ordered, Mark had projected them exactly to Tycho crater where he himself had originally arrived.

Claire, as she lay recovering and absorbing the incredible moonscape, watched the five men prowling around in the sunlight, busy with their detectors. At length they evidently found an area that satisfied them for they went to work with their fire-axes to chip away lava and pumice rock. Claire's eyes moved from them at last to the equipment they had brought, and particularly the few sticks of high explosive, which, as she knew, would detonate with shattering force under any sudden impact.

She thought a little further — even back to her own words to Mark when she had accused him of the murder of Harper. She had said, 'destroy or be destroyed.' And for some reason she found herself in Mark's place right now. This was only the beginning of the crumbling of his empire, unless she could smash it to pieces before it got out of hand.

In another twenty minutes the return to Earth would be made. She peered at her watch in a blinding edge of sunlight round the rock. Here on the moon, Mark had said, the gravity was only a sixth of the Earth's, therefore it should mean she could throw an object six times as far. It all depended on timing, too. She had no intention of blowing the men to pieces: she could not bring herself to do that; but she certainly might distract their attention at the most vital moment.

So when she was satisfied that they were too busy with their mining to notice her she glided out of her concealment to the equipment, carefully removed the high explosive sticks, and then returned to her former position. The shadow being inky she was invisible. She could make full use of the lack of sunlight diffraction — and did.

The twenty minutes required seemed

endless, but as they neared their climax and Baxter and his space-suited companions were preparing for the return walk towards the equipment, Claire acted. With every ounce of her strength, increased six times by the slight gravity, she hurled the sticks high over the heads of the men. Because she was in utter shadow they did not see her action — and also because the sticks were black against an inky sky they did not see them either. They travelled a seemingly incredible distance. Then followed a shattering explosion and spewing of pumice rock and dust towards the stars.

Claire waited tensely, wondering if her psychology were correct. It was. Baxter and his comrades, utterly astounded by an unexplained explosion on the moon, were impelled by sheer scientific interest in its direction. In vast leaps and bounds they raced towards the crater's edge and over a ridge.

Claire watched them go and then hurried over, to the crater's centre where the equipment and two specimen cases — already filled with samples, she noticed

— stood. At this moment the reversal beam clamped down upon her and she was catapulted into blackness. The next thing she realized was that brandy was being forced down her throat and Mark was bending over her.

'Okay?' he asked anxiously. 'Feel better?'

'Yes . . . much.' Claire stirred a little and found she was lying on the settee in the lounge, minus her spacesuit.

'You were knocked out when you came back,' Mark explained, as she propped herself on her elbow. 'And you came back alone, which I can't quite understand.'

'Then it worked,' Claire said, smiling bitterly.

'What did? What happened?'

Mark squatted down beside her.

'I ditched them, Mark — and without much effort, too.' She described in detail what she had done. 'The light gravity enabled me to throw the explosive for a prodigious distance, of course, and exactly as I'd hoped sheer curiosity made those five forget everything else and dash to investigate. It obviously never dawned on them that I might be responsible. They overlooked in doing that that they went beyond the area of the return beam, which you've explained to me so many times. So of course it didn't catch them up and bring them back. It wasn't murder, Mark — they just literally overstepped themselves.'

Mark smiled broadly and then delivered a resounding kiss.

'Long time since you had one of those,' he said, helping the girl to stand up. 'I never thought you had such resource. And what particularly pleases me is that we've got rid of all the annoying factions in one sweep. If there had been others they'd have joined in. Certainly they'll be dead by now. Their air would not last more than forty minutes at the very outside.'

'I don't — don't know whether I feel horror-stricken or not;' Claire mused. 'On the whole I think not. They didn't have to dash and investigate, did they?'

'Forget it,' Mark advised brusquely. 'It's over and done with. Incidentally, most of the equipment came back with you since it was in the area of the reversal beam. Two specimen cases with lunar mineral in them, too. Pretty valuable ore, I imagine, though I haven't tested it. Did you collect it?'

'No. It must have been one of the men. I was unconscious to begin with so I don't know what happened earlier.'

'Okay. I'll see what the few samples contain . . . and the crater is still ours, Claire — for if anything ever happens to me the lot goes to you. And I can see that, between us, we're going to beat all our enemies into the dust.'

5

Into the outer deeps

Despite Mark's confidence, however, he had an uncomfortable two weeks following the disappearance of Baxter and his colleagues. First, their disappearance from scientific circles was noticed; then Mount Wilson reported that five objects, later identified as spacesuited figures, had been located lying motionless in the crater of Tycho, and finally the law banged on Mark Rowland's door and asked for the facts.

He gave them to his legal adviser, and the legal adviser had a punishing task to make himself sound convincing. In the end his superior legal brilliance outshone the prosecution and it was generally conceded that Baxter and several other scientists had broken into Mark's home and fired themselves to the moon without thoroughly understanding the equipment.

Verification of the breaking in came from Mark's household staff, and the whole plot was also known to some lesser scientists who had refused to have anything to do with the notion when Baxter had tacitly suggested it to them. So, on this rather flat note, the storm died down and Mark emerged again, inwardly shaken but outwardly as dominant as ever.

The moment he was able he returned to his experiments to stabilize atomic aggregates and, at the end of two weeks, Claire was surprised one evening to find him jubilant. The moment she entered the laboratory he swept her off her feet in an excess of pleasure, then set her down beside the testing bench.

'Observe!' he ordered dramatically, and she looked at a dull grey sheet of metal about four inches square.

'Well, what is it?' she asked.

'The answer, m'dear! Or, more correctly, the catalyst I've been needing. Might as well call it lunarium, since it came from the moon.'

'It — what?' Claire looked puzzled.

'It is selected ore from those samples brought back from the moon when Baxter and his friends were wiped out. You remember the stuff in the specimen-cases? I analysed it recently, and then I found that some of it is just what I need to produce the exact vibration of copper needed for stabilizing atomic aggregates.'

'And — and it really works?'

'According to mathematics it does. It gets used up very fast in the process of transforming the copper, so I'll have to get some more from the moon as quickly as possible. On the journey I can find out if the stabilization is as good as I hope . . . I could almost thank Baxter for turning up as he did. Otherwise we might never have come across this stuff!'

Claire did not pursue the topic; she contented herself in being happy at Mark's triumph — and, as usual she stood by the equipment when, two nights later, he made his lunar trip for a large consignment of lunarium. He returned safely, as active as the moment when he had departed, a huge lined crate full of ores beside him.

'Perfect!' he exclaimed. 'Absolutely perfect! We've got it this time, Claire. It's like lying on a feather bed, and all that ghastly dropping is wiped out . . . '

'Then we're ready to hand it over to the public?'

'We soon shall be. First I must send men to the moon to obtain this lunarium in enormous quantities — which I can do since all the minerals in the crater are mine to do as I like with. That won't be difficult: the tough part will be to keep a watch on them that they don't steal the valuable stuff. Only way is to have each man examined when he comes back. I think I can find enough honest men to do the job.'

So Mark went to work through his many agents to secure a small army of fifty strong men, all willing to make the attempt. The pay was sufficient to tempt them and for many weeks thereafter, transitions were made back and forth and the resulting lunarium transferred to special storage depots, until at last Mark was satisfied there was enough to supply the dissembly termini for about a year. In any event he could always get more of the stuff whenever it was needed.

He did not stop at lunarium, however. Now that the Cosmic Engineers were established — for such was their title — he wanted to keep them. So he set up the Cosmos Mining Syndicate, in conjunction with those scientists who had turned down Baxter's plot — and thereby proved they were honest — and went to work to remove from the moon as rapidly as expedient all the valuable materials it contained. Inevitably it meant a share-out of wealth but this fact did not concern him particularly since he had come to realize that if he didn't get the stuff in the normal commercial way he would have it stolen. In this way the Cosmos Mining Syndicate was an 'offshoot' of the mighty E.T.C., which was now concerned solely in space-transitions to Mars for a big tourist majority.

Prosperity was definitely riding right for the E.T.C. The space-transition system grew steadily in popularity, and apart from the tourists there were the constant streams of scientists and astronomers who wished to bring their information concerning the red planet up to date. The moon was strictly out of bounds whilst the Mining Syndicate was at work.

In another two years the E.T.C. was the dominating commercial concern of the world. By this time the lunar mining was over and all the most valuable elements extracted. How much he was worth Mark did not know. Probably he was one of the richest men in the world. The fact pleased him, but it was not his only thought. He was still desirous of reaching further — so he experimented by hurling himself to Venus, in a specially reinforced globe akin to a bathysphere, to protect him from the atmospheric pressure. Once again was hailed as a hero as he returned with first-hand observations, taken by instruments of a hellishly-hot cloud-sheathed world akin to Dante's Inferno. The planet appeared lifeless, but scientists and geologists were fascinated, and there was a steady demand for space-transition tickets from some of the more daring scientists and explorers.

So the tentacles spread, and every time Mark himself had the courage to make the initial journeys. Further and further he flung himself, exploring the way. Jupiter was an even more dangerous planet. It was a world suitable only for remote-controlled television cameras and robotic instruments, and that was all. E.T.C. could not guarantee safety on Jupiter.

Neither were Saturn, Uranus, and Neptune recommend by Mark for adding to the 'visitation' list. They were mainly gaseous, with poisonous ammonia-charged atmospheres. No human beings could possibly survive the 500-m.p.h. hurricanes that often screamed round the giant worlds. However, all of the outer planets had rocky satellites, several of them of dimensions comparable to the Earth's Moon, and it was to these moons that parties of daring astronomers ventured, in order to make direct observations of the giant planets. The secrets of planetary creation were being opened up to science, and Mark was hailed as the genius who had brought it about.

Pluto was a possibility for those who wished to view the face of infinity from the rim of the Solar System. It was a dark, rocky, utterly desolated world, but nevertheless it was put on the list . . . So, for the time being, Mark came to a halt.

For a while he juggled with the idea of seeing what Mercury had to offer, and then in the face of the overwhelming astronomical evidence concerning it he decided against it. Its proximity to the dangerous radiations of the sun made it a deathtrap for human beings, however well protected. But robots and scientific equipment could still be sent, and were. So, for the time being, Mark came to a halt. Surprised to find that there were no more worlds left to conquer.

What then? Only the outer deeps at which he had gazed during his brief visit to Pluto. It was plain the vision splendid had impressed him for he frequently referred to it to Claire as the months flew by.

'But why can't you be satisfied with what you have, Mark?' This was invariably her ceaseless plea. 'We are worth all the money we can possibly need: E.T.C. is on the very crest of prosperity. The entire Solar System can be reached in an instant, thanks to you. Why not leave well alone and rest on your laurels?'

'It is not in me to rest, m'dear,' Mark answered her.

They were seated together on the broad terrace of their home. It was summer and the evening was calm, as calm indeed as their lives had been for several months now. So firmly were they established in their chosen way of life there were few things that could concern them. But they were becoming older. It showed in the increased sedateness of their movements and the grey touch in their hair.

'I should be a fool,' Mark said, 'to stop at Pluto when my transition system gives me the whole universe to play with. I want to contact other beings, make interplanetary communication really possible.'

'Why?' Claire asked, with a patient glance.

'Why not? I've drawn a blank so far. Every planet in the Solar System bar

Earth is uninhabited. I refuse to believe that this world of ours is the only one, amidst the infinite myriads of planets, possessing intelligent life. I want to find other intelligences, if only for the purpose of establishing a universal brotherhood.'

Claire laughed softly. 'Oh, how well I know you, Mark! You have no desire to establish a brotherhood: your sole ambition is to dominate, and you won't be happy until you have found populated worlds which must do exactly as you order.'

'All right, have it that way if you like. There certainly isn't much fun in just having this one planet doing as you tell it — for that's pretty well what it has come to these days. I have such tremendous influence that Governments act as I tell them. And so far nobody's suffered . . . But it won't do. I'm not an old man yet and I must go further.'

'I have the instinctive feeling that you shouldn't,' Claire warned.

'Woman's intuition?' He got to his feet. 'That's bunk, Claire. There isn't such a thing. And I've got to have some action!'

Leaving her, he went into the house and to the visiphone. In a matter of seconds he had been connected to Dr. Willard Prior, the chief of the British Astronomical Association.

'Oh, hello Mark!' Prior's rubicund, genial face appeared on the screen. 'Anything the matter?'

'Not particularly the matter, but I'd like to ask you a few questions. Sorry to drag you out of your home at this hour in the evening, but can you come over?'

'Surely — be glad to. Wife's away on holiday, as a matter of fact, so it'll break the monotony. Be with you in quarter of an hour.'

'Thanks.' Mark switched off and returned to Claire on the terrace. He told her briefly what he had done and then had the manservant fetch another chair and refreshment in readiness for Prior's arrival.

'But what do you want with him?' Claire asked.

'You'll see . . . Meanwhile, have a drink.'

Mark poured out sherry and he and

Claire were just about finishing their drinks when Prior arrived. He came on to the terrace from the driveway, smiling genially, and shook hands.

'He's smitten with the urge to explore again,' Claire sighed. 'It's as simple as that.'

Mark grinned. 'Claire's been married to me long enough to know I can't stay put, Willard. And you know it, too. I wanted to ask you: does Pluto exhaust the Solar System for exploration?'

'I'm afraid it does. Unless any of the recently discovered minor planets and cometary fragments scattered beyond Pluto — itself a minor planet — interest you?'

'Not a bit . . . All right, then, where's the next nearest real planet beyond our solar system?'

'Well now,' Prior answered thoughtfully, 'there is no other planet within normal telescopic observation — but according to mathematics and our latest detection systems, there is one, or maybe several, like those of our own Solar System, gravitating around Alpha Centauri. They are appreciable only by perturbations in the motion of Alpha himself, and the only explicable reason is the presence of a planet, or planets. In my view I think there is only one planet, and that is of considerable dimensions, using Alpha Centauri as its sun.'

'And that's the best we can do?' Mark asked.

'Afraid so. You're really in the outer deeps when you talk about Alpha Centauri. He's twenty-five billion miles away, remember, and it would take more than four years to reach him, even moving at the speed of light.'

Mark considered. 'You say this hypothetical planet is entirely invisible?'

'Unfortunately, yes. Even Mount Wilson can't spot him, and they have the best reflector and the best climate in the world for observation.'

'Suppose an extremely brilliant flash were produced upon him — the planet I mean — such as we have produced on Pluto and other worlds for test purposes, could it be seen? Using, say, an H-bomb instead of conventional chemical explosives?'

'I doubt it,' Prior replied. 'The distance is colossal, you must remember. In any case, man, you can't do it. Sending an H-bomb to this hypothetical planet is right out of the question, unless you are prepared to wait nearly nine years to see the flash!'

'Answer the question,' Mark insisted. 'Could the flash be seen?'

'I don't believe it could, no. Even Alpha himself, a large star of the first magnitude, is little more than a speck in the mightiest telescope, so it is hard to imagine how the flash of an H-bomb on an infinitely smaller planet could be spotted. In any case the radiance of Alpha would be greater than the flash and would drown it . . . But we're talking about wonderland!' Prior objected. 'You can't reach that far, Mark, so forget it!'

'Supposing,' Mark said, musing, 'powerful telescopic equipment was transferred to Pluto, how then? In a sealed dome? You'd be three thousand three hundred million miles nearer to Alpha than you are on Earth here. How then?'

'Yes, we'd see it then I believe,' Prior

assented, his rubicund face astonished. 'Definitely so. There's no air on Pluto and we'd have a completely spatial view right across infinity, and we'd be appreciably nearer the objective . . . Just what are you getting at?'

'Just this. I feel like taking an extreme leap into the outer deeps. If the planet of Alpha can be reached in a reasonable length of time, then so can any planet in the whole Universe. Out to the First Galaxy, onwards to — '

'The limiting factor of the speed of light prevents you making such a leap!' Prior insisted. 'Fitzgerald's Contraction says — '

'That a body exceeding the speed of light becomes minus-zero and therefore nothing,' Mark interrupted. 'Yes, I know. But that is only what Fitzgerald says.'

'He's never been proven wrong!'

'Nobody has had any reason to do so yet. For myself, I never could see why there should be a limiting speed to waves of light. There isn't to thought-waves, which are in the same order of radiation only infinitely shorter in wavelength, so why to light? Thought can jump from here to Pluto — or anywhere — in a split second. Correct?'

'I admit thought has no barriers, but this is different. You are talking of an atomic parcel being projected — '

'I am, yes, but I am thinking of breaking it down into a very different wavelength to the one usually used. In other words, reducing it to a wavelength that corresponds to that of thought wavelength. That is known to be shorter than cosmic waves, hence its tremendous power which carries it through solids. It comes to this, Willard. The shorter the wavelength, the less liable it is to be governed by Fitzgerald's Law.'

Prior was silent for a long time and Claire glanced from him to her husband.

'An atomic parcel of that wavelength would produce light-waves also of an unusual order,' Mark added. 'They would be as instantaneous as the transition.'

'Well,' Prior said, 'if you think you can reduce a giant H-bomb to ultra-short wavelength so it will travel infinitely faster than light, good luck to you. If it succeeds you'll have proved that light is not the limit of speed. Now, regarding this Plutonian observatory, are you serious?'

'Definitely, and I'll do it at my own expense. If I succeed in making so colossal a trip, then I will inform the world and to the E.T.C. I shall add the Universe-Transition Line. That way I'll make my money back a thousand-fold . . . Don't you see, man, this faraway world can become a stepping-stone. From there I can leap further and further.'

'Maybe we'd better try and deal with this one first,' Prior suggested, catching a hopeless look from Claire. 'Now, about this Plutonian observatory, what exactly do you want done?'

'Well, first I'll send the Cosmic Engineers to build the observatory, complete with all living quarters and so forth — and of course sealed off front the interstellae void. Your particular task will be to duplicate the Mount Wilson apparatus and then it can be dispatched by the usual transition system to its out-post . . . But come inside and we'll discuss,' Mark said. 'It's getting chilly out here.'

★　★　★

So, in the months that followed, the giant reflector of Mount Wilson was copied in exact detail, and most of the resources of precision and lens engineering were thrown into the job. The normal cooling of the giant lenses, which would have taken over two years with grinding and polishing, was shortened by high-speed processes that in no wise detracted from the efficiency of fine focus.

Mark himself supervised most of this activity, whilst from Pluto the Cosmic Engineers sent word that the observatory was taking rapid shape on a lonely mountain peak from which the great maw of infinity loomed uninterrupted.

Altogether, Mark was a satisfied and extremely busy man, for apart from keeping a check on others he had also his own work to do — that of controlling the affluent destiny of E.T.C., and also working out mathematically the new dissembling wavelength so that it approached the short-wave penetration of thought itself. With mathematical computing machines and his scientific genius to help him he solved the problem in six months, by which time the great reflector intended for Pluto was ready, complete on its electrically geared mountings — and on Pluto itself the observatory was ready to receive it.

The transfer of the mighty reflector was made without publicity. Only Mark, Claire, Ted Shepley, and Willard Prior knew about it. As ever, Mark was determined not to breathe a word about his experiments until he had proved them successful: in this way he kept the breath of failure constantly away from his celebrated name. One or two tourist groups did wonder why certain parts of Pluto had been put out of bounds, but this was the only clue.

Mark and Willard Prior made the transition themselves to Pluto to watch the assembly of the equipment and check over the work done — then, satisfied that everything was as it should be under the air-tight dome and that radio with Earth was working satisfactorily, Mark returned home and left Prior in charge. Four expert astronomers were sent to aid him, and so, radio link-up complete, the evening came round for the transition of a gigantic H-bomb, fully six feet in length and loaded to capacity with explosive, to be 'transitized' to Alpha Centauri's lonely planet.

In the interval exact mathematics had determined that there was only one planet, and not several, and that it was about the size and mass of Jupiter. Its position was perfectly known and all the relevant equations concerning it had been plotted on the computers. All that remained now, on the stroke of 8-0 p.m., was for Mark to give the order.

Claire was with him in the private laboratory, gazing in some apprehension at the vast bomb under the magnets, whilst the radio-television carried the voice and image of Ted Shepley in the master control-room of London's leading T.R. station. Pluto was also linked up and Prior had already given assurance that Alpha-Minor — as the solitary planet was now named — was under continuous observation.

'I still feel you shouldn't do it, Mark,'

Claire said, her eyes on the sweep-hand of the clock. 'You're reaching too far. You just don't know when to stop!'

'Oh, don't hand me that woman's intuition stuff now!' he snapped. 'I've too much on my mind — Okay, Ted, you ready?'

'Yes — and I hope you know we'll be using nearly thirty-million e-volts for this projection. The distance and your new dissembly method accounts for it.'

'That doesn't signify. I don't care if we soak the city dry of power for the time being: this experiment goes through. Right! Five seconds to go.'

Mark began to count montonously. 'Four — three — two — one — Over!' and he slammed in the dissembly switch.

The bomb vanished almost instantly instead of slowly, under the new type of dissembly. Three seconds later the lights in the laboratory dimmed for a moment and then went out; to come up again as the emergency circuit came into action.

'On its way!' came the voice of Ted. 'Can't estimate the speed. Prior will have to figure that one out — All lights have been put out, except emergency circuits. There'll be a row over that.'

'Damn that,' Mark answered tersely — but just the same, for the next five minutes, he was kept busy answering emergency calls to know if he could explain the sudden power failure. He denied all responsibility, and finally was relieved from excuses as power returned to normal after the vast drain which had been momentary made upon it.

'This is the part I don't like,' Mark muttered, pacing the laboratory like a caged tiger whilst Claire patiently watched him. 'Aiming at an object so far away the naked eye can't see it, having to rely on other people to tell you something. If I hadn't have had to stay here to dispatch the bomb I'd have gone to Pluto.'

He roamed again, smoking innumerable cigarettes, then after a long interval he sprang to the radio equipment as Prior's voice came through. It was tense and incredulous. Mark thought briefly of the cosmic paradox implicit in the message: the transition of the bomb to Alpha had probably taken less time than

Prior's message — sent from Pluto via normal radio waves — to reach the Earth.

'You did it, Mark! You actually did it. A minute or so ago we saw a distinct spot of light — so brief we hardly saw it. But the photographic equipment got it. Here's what we got. Over.'

The television came into action and, though the vast distance distorted the scene, somewhat, there was a distinct vision of a tiny pinprick of light amidst a dimly discernable circle.

'Then light is *not* limited by Fitzgerald!' Mark exclaimed, jubilant. 'We can cross any distance in a reasonable time. Exactly when did you get the flash? Over.'

Thereafter there followed long intervals whilst Prior's observational results were transmitted from Pluto, and received and analyzed by Mark back on Earth. Eventually the data was complete, and Mark was jubilant.

'That means it took that bomb seven and a half minutes to cross the gulf, and seven and a half minutes for the new-type wavelengths to be rebounded. Seven and a half minutes — no, not quite. They were received then on Pluto, which knocks a good deal of time off. Anyway we can work that out later. The fact remains, it can be done.' He shot a glance at Ted Shepley, who was looking thoughtful. 'Anything the matter, Ted?'

'According to Prior's observations, that must have been one hell of an explosion,' he said slowly. 'It probably blasted to atoms much of the planet concerned!'

'What does that matter?' Mark asked brusquely. 'All right, we've learned all we want to know. I'll find our next if that planet — or what remains of it — is a possible place to visit. If so we'll open up our new transit-system to the further reaches. I'll make the attempt tomorrow night. Meantime, Ted, stay in touch with Willard because he'll be needed again.'

'You can rely on it,' Ted promised, and moved to the radio equipment.

Smiling, Mark turned to where Claire was seated.

'As simple as that,' he said, spreading his hands. I hope you realize, m'dear, that apart from the actual conquest of inconceivable distance I have also brought a new law of physics into being concerning the speed of light. For that my name will be bracketed with Max Planek, Einstein, and sundry others of scientific history.'

'Uh-huh,' Claire assented, by no means enthusiastic.

'What the devil's the matter with you?' Mark demanded. 'I at least rate something better than a grunt, don't I?'

'Sorry, Mark.' Claire got to her feet. 'I — I just haven't taken it all in yet, and I'm still overwhelmed by that funny feeling that you shouldn't have done it.'

'Oh, stop talking rubbish! Come along into the house. We need to celebrate after this lot! And tomorrow night, this time with you at the controls, I'll make the biggest leap ever — to Alpha Minor. Twenty-five billion miles!'

6

Retribution

Mark and Claire, like most people on the night-side of Earth, retired to bed in the normal way and were soon asleep. At least Mark was, not in the least over-excited by the scientific miracles he had performed during the evening.

But for Claire sleep did not come easily. She lay long after midnight staring wakefully at the rectangle of window, against which the night was coldly bright. It was late autumn now, with a distinct bite of frost in the air.

Because she was awake she saw the pallid glare that lit the heavens momentarily towards two in the morning, and a few seconds later she heard a remote concussion that made the window rattle slightly. She frowned to herself. Evidently a meteorite, by no means uncommon in the autumn, but it sounded to have been of stupendous size.

Then as she lay thinking it out the heavens brightened again, and once more there was a reverberation, nearer this time. It made the ornaments on the dressing table clink slightly. That got Claire out of bed quickly. One giant meteorite was possible, but two — and in quick succession — was phenomenal. In a few seconds she was in her gown and slippers and reached the window, just in time to see an unholy light belching out of the upper heavens. Simultaneously there came a screaming roar as though a jet-plane were streaking over the residence at only a hundred feet. For split seconds, her eyes dazzled with the fiendish light, Claire caught a glimpse of something spherical, then it whistled over the horizon.

And this time, the explosion and shock was paralyzing. It blew the window in on top of her, the blast hurling her backwards. She felt vicious barbs tear into her face as she reeled in the showering glass and then struck the dressing table. At the same instant the room rocked, the ceiling cracked, and she screamed help-lessly as tumbling clouds of brick and masonry thundered down on top of her.

Mark, who had awakened at the screaming whistle, found himself flung out of the bed and into a corner, but he escaped the main downdrop of the room. When the earthquake effects had abated slightly he staggered to his feet and went across to where Claire was unconscious and bleeding amidst the wreckage. He could dimly see her in the starlight — and for a second or two he saw her even more brightly as another of the fiendish unknowns roared terrifyingly through the sky and landed with appalling force somewhere in the midst of London.

The wrecked room rocked and swayed. More masonry came down. Mark tugged savagely and at last dragged Claire free. With her in his arms he reeled to the door and out into the long passage beyond. The house was full of noise from drunken wails, the cries of hastily dressed servants, and the sound of fractured waterpipes, spouting viciously.

'Mr. Rowland, what's happening?'

cried the butler, hurrying up. 'Is it an earthquake, war, or what — ?'

'No idea,' Mark retorted. 'My wife's badly knocked about. I'm taking her outside. May be safer out there. All of you come with me . . . and get the first aid kit.'

Grabbing a rug on the way for covering. Mark hurried into the grounds and laid Claire down. It gradually dawned upon him, as the servants crowded around and endeavoured to help, that the lights in the sky had ceased. But, in various directions on the faraway horizons, were flickering red glows that told their own grim story. Just what had happened Mark did not know: he was nearly too anxious to think.

'Claire,' he whispered, wiping the blood from her ashy face with a wet sponge. 'Claire, it's me — Mark. We're all safe now.'

At the sound of his voice she revived a little. 'Speak — speak for yourself, Mark,' she whispered. 'I'm finished, and I know it.'

'Don't be so absurd, m'dear. Cuts from glass and — '

'More than that. That masonry crushed me. I — funny thing, Mark. Dad always said you'd sacrifice even me, and you have.'

'Huh?' Mark demanded. 'What did you say?' Claire did not answer. She was motionless in his arms. It took him several seconds, and a brief examination, to discover that she was dead . . . He did not quite know what to do after that. The next cold-sober thoughts he had were when he was in the half-demolished remains of the lounge, a shirt and trousers roughly pulled into shape about him, whilst he waited for Dr. Latham, his usual physician, to state the reason for death. He did so when at length he came into the temporarily candle-lit room.

'Sorry, Mark,' he said quietly. 'Even if I'd got here sooner I couldn't have done anything. Broken ribs had penetrated her heart, and there were other severe injuries.

'Why did it have to happen?' Mark yelled in fury. 'What the devil's been going on? Those explosions?'

'No idea. I heard them, same as you,

and my house is in bad shape. I think we can call ourselves fortunate that we're outside the main city limits because London seemed to catch it pretty badly. Must be war and atom bombs. Can't be anything else,' Mark stood with his fists clenched, looking about him — then he turned as the butler came dimly into sight.

'Well, what is it?' Mark demanded

'The visiphone in the laboratory is buzzing for attention. There doesn't seem to be much damage in there.'

'Thanks.' Mark clapped Dr. Latham briefly on the shoulder. 'And thank you too, Doc. I'll get myself under control in a bit.'

Mark went on his way through the shaken desolation of the residence and into the annex where the laboratory lay. As the butler had said, the laboratory had survived the main onslaught and the emergency light was on. Taut-faced, Mark switched on the visiphone and Ted Shepley's worried visage appeared.

'Mark, the very devil's happened!' he exclaimed, shaken.

'As if I didn't know,' Mark told him sourly. 'Claire's been killed by the collapse of this blasted house.'

'Claire — dead? Oh no, Mark!'

'I tell you she is! What do you want, anyway? I'm in no mood to speak to anybody.'

'Afraid you've got to. For your information four massive atomic bombs, or something like it, have dropped in and around London. The damage is appalling and the death roll is beyond computation at the moment. Three of our T.R. stations have gone skywards, but the main one is still intact. I'm speaking from there now. Ambulances and rescue squads are at work everywhere . . .

'Then it's war?' Mark asked grimly.

'I don't know. I can't believe that it is, somehow. Our Intelligence couldn't be so utterly in the dark about it starting — '

'I tell you it's war!' Mark stated flatly. 'Guided missiles! What the devil else could it be?'

'It could be . . . Alpha Minor.'

'What?' Mark asked, his tone curiously quiet.

'I said it could be Alpha Minor. Truth to tell I've been wondering for some time about the advisibility of firing bombs to other worlds just to see the flash. Fortunately you've hit uninhabited worlds until now ... Now it looks like that six-foot atomic H-bomb of yours landed smack in the middle of a scientific civilization and they didn't like it. So they have fired some back!'

'Rubbish!' Mark said flatly.

'I hope it is, because if it isn't we may get dozens more of 'em. These few may be to test the range ... Y'know, poor Claire often said heaven help us if you ever dropped a bomb on folks able to hit back ...'

'She did? M'm, so that's what she meant.'

'Meant?' Ted's face was surprised on the screen.

'Yes. Just before she died she said I'd sacrifice her. I couldn't understand her then. Now I know what she meant. She must have guessed that these things might be retaliation from Alpha Minor, and that if I'd not reached out so far, as she asked me not to, it would never have happened.'

There was an uncomfortable silence; then Ted said, 'I'm probably wrong. There'll be ultimata over the radio soon from our enemies and then we'll know it's just plain war again.'

'I'll see you tomorrow, or rather later today,' Mark said, and switched off. He just could not talk any more. He was too choked up with emotions of rage and grief.

War? Alpha Minor hitting back? By the time the frosty dawn came he and the rest of the world knew the worst as radio stations gave out their grim story. It was not war, for various countries, including those of Britain's own enemies, had been blasted by titanic explosions. Some had occurred in open country and others in densely populated areas. Out of the sky mammoth bombs had descended and, only an hour before the radio reports came through, two had fallen in Australia — explained by that side of the globe now being turned towards Alpha Minor.

The howl of dismay which went up from the populations of the world was tremendous, but questioning did not immediately turn upon Mark since nobody outside his immediate associates knew about his experiment with Alpha Minor — and whilst he did his best to get his thoughts straightened out he had the chance to bury Claire, with full civic honors.

This done he returned to the struggle, somewhat cheered by the fact that the bombs had ceased to drop. After those on Australia no more had arrived, so perhaps the retaliatory onslaught, if such it were, was over.

Just the same, the finger was now pointing to him, chiefly because Ted Shepley had opened his mouth rather too wide and told the Government of the Alpha Minor experiment and that, in his view, this was retaliation for Mark overstepping himself. The first Mark heard about it was an order to appear at Government headquarters and explain things. He had to comply, but he did not go direct. He stopped at the E.T.C. headquarters in the midst of the shattered city and walked in on Ted Shepley as he did his best to handle the work usually controlled by Claire.

'Hello, Mark!' He glanced up briefly from the desk. 'Getting over the shock?'

'If you mean about Claire, yes. If you mean about yourself, no.'

'About me?' Ted looked surprised. 'What's the matter with me?'

'Everything,' Mark retorted, crossing, to the desk and sitting down. 'By what damned right did you take it on yourself to inform the Government of our Alpha Minor, experiment?'

'What else could I do in order to be honest? Experts have checked the remains of the bombs that descended upon us and have come to the conclusion that they were never made on this planet, but by scientists infinitely ahead of us in engineering and knowledge of armaments. As chief engineer of E.T.C. I was asked if I could identify them as perhaps belonging to belligerents on Mars or Venus — scientists trying scare tactics to wrest control of Earth. Naturally I had to squash such fantastic notions, so I explained that they probably came from Alpha Minor.'

'Very helpful of you,' Mark sneered. 'Why couldn't you have let them go on thinking they might be from some hidden race on Mars or Venus? Give the interplanetary Intelligence some work to do for a change. As it is you've got me on the carpet.'

'I'm sorry about that, but it seems to me they'd have found out about it sooner or later — '

'No reason why they should since they didn't know a thing about the experiment.' Mark's face hardened. 'You've been wanting to get me in a spot, Ted, ever since that night I pushed Harper out of our way. I suppose you think you owe it to your conscience, or some such rot. Fact remains I've no use for a man who can betray a private experiment that easily, and without even consulting my wishes first.'

Ted sprang to his feet. 'Look here, Mark, I — '

'I'm looking, and I don't like what I see. I consider you're not to be trusted, Ted, and once I feel that way you might as well quit. And I mean now. I'll tell the

Sub-Bank to work out exactly how much is due and it will be forwarded later today.'

Ted hesistated, his lips tight. Then he asked quietly, 'And this is all our friendship means to you?'

'Our friendship ceased the night Harper died. I saw it in your face and I've wondered ever since when you'd sneak in and hit back.'

Ted said no more. He collected a few belongings from the desk drawer and then turned and left the office. Mark reached to the intercom and switched on. It was the sub-chief of the London T.R. stations who appeared on the tiny screen.

'Yes, Mr. Rowland?'

'You're taking over here in headquarters in place of Shepley,' Mark said. 'He's resigned.'

The sub-chief did not show that he was surprised. 'When am I to commence duties, sir?'

'Immediately. Come right over and transfer your present duties to Marsden. I'll wait for you.'

Mark switched off, wandering about

the office and pausing presently for a moment beside the window. For a moment even his conscience was stirred as he gazed at the wilderness of ruins created by the mystery-bombs. Then he deliberately turned his back upon the havoc and prepared the various papers with which Carson, the former sub-chief, would have to deal with when he arrived.

Presently he presented himself. Mark gave him the necessary details and then departed for Government headquarters. They were only temporary since the original seat of Government had been blown to powder. Nor was it the prime minister who was present, he having been wiped out in the destruction of his home. In charge now was Governor Hillman and his associates, who were also responsible for the military side of the situation.

Mark could sense the feelings towards him the moment he entered the office. He took a seat as the Governor motioned.

'I suppose, Mr. Rowland, you are aware of the circumstances?' the Governor asked. 'That this city and several others, together with a lot of fortunately empty tracts of land, have been subjected to violent bombardment as an act of retaliation?'

'The act of retaliation being suggested by Mr. Shepley?' Mark asked.

'Exactly.'

'Have you any other proof?'

'We have no proof at all. Only his word for it — and it sounds reasonable.'

'Maybe so, but it is completely at variance with the facts. Mr. Shepley allowed his imagination to run away with him.'

The Governor pondered and glanced briefly at his associates.

'Alpha Minor,' Mark said deliberately, 'is twenty-five billion miles away. Light from Alpha Centauri, the sun of Alpha Minor, takes more than four years to reach us . . . How then can you possibly imagine that bombs could be thrown at us from there, only a few hours after my experiment?'

'Yes, there's logic in that,' one of the men agreed.

'Thanks,' Mark replied cynically.

161

'On the other hand,' Governor Hillman commented, 'you succeeded in hurling your test bomb to this — er — Alpha Minor in only a few minutes. We have a report from Willard Prior, stationed on Pluto, to that effect.'

Mark's expression changed. So he had been talking, too! 'Did he volunteer that information?' he asked.

'He gave it after we had radioed to him. Naturally the Government is fully aware of your Plutonian activities . . . What I am driving at,' the Governor continued grimly, 'is that if you could send a missile to Alpha Minor in so short a time, then they could probably send some back at the same velocity. We have got it on good authority that the bombs they hurled at us are the products of an extremely advanced science, so doubtless distance does not form a barrier to their activities.'

Mark spread his hands. 'Believe me, Governor, I'm as worried about this ghastly business as anybody, but you can't hold me responsible for it — always assuming Alpha Minor is the real cause. No dissenting voice was raised when I hurled explosives at Mars, the moon, and Venus. Why now?'

'There are always dissenting voices, Mr. Rowland, when somebody gets hurt. The damage and loss of life has been appalling, of course, but fortunately the bombs seem to have stopped falling. We asked you here in case they resume. If they do, it is your duty to project yourself to Alpha Minor and apologize, as well as you can to strange beings, for your behavior and explain how it came about.'

Mark flushed angrily. 'Are you giving me orders?'

'Yes,' Hillman answered flatly. 'The public demand it — but only if attack is resumed. You should remember, Mr. Rowland, that a man only retains his popularity as long as he benefits humanity. The moment he appears to do the opposite — no matter how technically innocent he may be — he's ruined. That's how it is now. The world knows, though not very directly perhaps, that your efforts to reach a far distant planet have resulted in untold damage to ourselves. You are cited variously as ambitious, ruthless, and a killer. I am just giving you a chance to put things straight if the need still arises.'

Mark got to his feet, his face cold. 'That all, Governor?'

'That is all, Mr. Rowland, yes.'

Mark took his departure and returned home — or to what was left of it. Here he spent some time considering the situation in which he found himself; then finally he went into the laboratory and switched on the radio equipment. He transmitted a message through to Willard Prior requesting that he and the Cosmic Engineers readied themselves to be transferred back home to Earth.

Mark switched off and considered, then he moved to the normal radio apparatus which would put him in touch with Carson, now taking the place of Ted Shepley. At length Carson appeared in the telescreen.

'You know enough about major power loads to handle a Pluto transfer, don't you?' Mark questioned.

'I do, sir.'

'Right. Stand by for one in — ' Mark glanced at the clock, 'fifty-eight minutes precisely. I'll contact you again.'

'Right, sir.'

Mark switched off and began his preparations, but he had scarcely started before the visiphone shrilled for attention. He snatched up the instrument impatiently.

'Yes? Mark Rowland speaking . . . '

'Bad news, Mr. Rowland,' came the voice of Governor Hillman. 'Information has just been received that the bombs have begun again, and in far greater numbers than before. They seem to be peppering all parts of the night-side of Earth indiscriminately.'

'And you expect me now to go to Alpha Minor?' Mark demanded.

'I do.'

'Sorry, but I refuse to do it. In fact I can't. The only person who understood the controls well enough to handle them and project me was my wife. I made her my special student. I can't trust myself to anybody else.'

'I think you'd better, Mr. Rowland. Even a person you can't trust at the controls is better than an enraged mob looking for you — for that's what it will come to if the bombs start dropping here.'

'Which is a polite way of telling me to go out and hang myself?'

'It's up to you, Mr. Rowland. Either way you're in a pretty unpleasant situation.'

'I'm staying right here. I'd sooner be blown up with bombs than stick my neck out at a race of super-scientists.'

'Up to you, as I said before. Seems to me your curiosity has turned into a boomerang.'

Mark switched off savagely, then as he reflected his expression slowly altered.

'Boomerang?' he repeated, looking up and around him.

'Boomerang? By heaven, I wonder! One slim chance to put myself back on the pedestal and smash this retaliation onslaught to bits.'

The idea that had been born could not be developed there and then for he had his preparations to finish for the return of Willard Prior and his colleagues. So he completed them, and at the given time, perfectly controlled, the astronomer and his comrades merged into view under the magnets. Mark heaved a sigh of relief and shook hands.

'I want you to stay, Willard,' he said. 'Something I must ask you. You other fellows are free to return home — and if your homes have vanished apply to Governor Hillman for information regarding temporary living quarters.'

The astronomers nodded their thanks and departed. Prior gave Mark a questioning look, then accepted the drink of restorative which was handed to him.

'I'd rather like to get home myself, Mark,' he remarked. 'I'm worried as to what may have happened to my family.'

'Your family's okay: I checked on that. And your home too — and you are the only person with whom I can discuss an idea which has just come to me. Take a seat on the stool; that's it. Now, I think you ought to know that the bombs have started again. They're raining down on the night-side of Earth, according to Governor Hillman.'

Prior gave him a grim look. 'They are,

167

eh? So what happens now? Do you go to Alpha Minor?'

'I do not, and I've told the Governor as much. Anyway, I can't because nobody understands the controls well enough to send me. Claire used to do that — '

'I could learn quickly.'

'No doubt, but I'm not doing it. No, what I propose to do is produce the masterpiece of my career and put myself right back in the public eye as its great benefactor.'

'Doing what?'

'Throwing the bombs straight back to Alpha Minor.'

Prior was tired and he gave an impatient look. 'What in blazes do you think this is? A cosmic tennis match?'

'I'm not being facetious, Willard. I think I can boomerang this hail of bombs so they'll not only not hit us, but go right back to where they came from.'

'Well, of course, if you could — ' Prior put down his glass. 'How in blazes do you propose to do it?'

'It's radio again,' Mark said, beginning to prowl and hitting at the air to emphasize his points. 'You're an astrono-mer by profession, Willard, but you're also a physicist, of sorts, aren't you?'

'I can try and follow you anyway.'

'Right! Then follow this: an object travelling is generating energy. Elemen-tary?'

'Definitely.'

'Then what happens if a powerful dis-torting electrical field feeds the expended energy straight back into the moving object?' Prior frowned and groped mentally; then astonishment crossed his face.

'Hell's bells. You'd stop the object dead in its tracks and it would move in the opposite direction at precisely the same speed as it came, due to the energy being identical, but in the reverse order.'

'That's it,' Mark said. 'It's purely a radio field with alterations, but the greatest screen ever devised. What I am going to do is rig up a model effect, and if it works I'm going further — much further. That's why I want you, to give me a hand.'

Prior did not hesitate, though he had not much idea what he was about. He

169

helped with general gadgetry and watched Mark's skilled hands at work on electrical devices, until at last he had rigged up something that looked like a radio aerial between two rods, and connected to transformers and the normal power-plug.

'Now,' Mark murmured, rubbing his hands. 'This is it. We might try a ball first.'

He produced a tennis ball from amidst his junk drawer, then with the apparatus switched on he went to a position twelve feet distant and hurled the ball straight at the equipment. As though the ball had hit a rubber belt it shot straight back into his hand at exactly the same angle and exactly the same speed at which it had started forward.

'You've got it!' Prior cried, blinking in surprise.

'We'll make sure — dead sure,' Mark said, and picked up a revolver from the wall rack. He had kept it there ever since the altercation with Dean Baxter. He rigged it up on a portable stand with string to the trigger: then he fired it. There was an almost instantaneous report as the bullet exploded — in the gun itself!

'Hence the string,' Mark grinned, 'otherwise I might have blown my hand off. You couldn't see what happened because the bullet travelled so fast, but it means that it hit the recoiling field, had its energy slapped back straight into it, and so flew straight back into the gun barrel and exploded. Yes, we have it! And can we give these awkward master-minds on Alpha Minor something to think about from here on.'

'But, man alive, what do you propose doing? These smalltime experiments with a recoiling field are one thing, but protecting the whole world is definitely another. Think of the power you'll need!'

'I need no more than the power I have right here in this small instrument.'

Prior stared, wondering if the strain of events had at last unbalanced Mark's brilliant mind.

'Around this planet at about twenty miles up is the Heaviside Layer,' Mark continued. 'It is, of course, a mass of ions which will easily carry electrical current of any type. Charge one small section of the ionized layer with this particular distorting electrical field, and the remaining ions throughout the Layer will almost immediately alter to the same current by chain reaction of the ions. In brief, a few seconds power from this will be sufficient to make the entire Heaviside Layer as we want it.'

'But even then, Mark, there won't be enough power to stop bombs smashing through.'

Mark gave an impatient glance. 'Haven't you realized yet, man, that the power of repulsion is generated by the objects themselves? Their own energy is flung back into them — and since they must have crossed space at a speed far greater than that of light, they will automatically go back at the same speed, unexploded, until they reach their starting point. The Heaviside Layer will only have the recoiling field, which is almost as negligible in itself as a net to a tennis ball.'

'Pity we shan't be able to see the result of this boomerang business,' Prior remarked. 'But with light waves at normal speed the effect won't be known for four years.'

'I wouldn't count on that.' Mark thought for a moment. 'These bombs are obviously made by brilliant scientists, otherwise they would not cross space at their inconceivable speed. It is possible that their explosive force may generate light waves that will also flash across space at a speed greatly in excess of what Fitzgerald's Law says. Like my special bomb. If that should be so we'll see plenty, I hope! And so will the world. However, time's getting on and we've things to do. This gadget of mine has to be taken into the Heaviside Layer, or just below it, and there be released — or rather the current of it. Simple enough from the power-plant of a radio-guided projectile.'

Mark wasted no more time. He switched on the visiphone and contacted Governor Hillman. When he saw the caller on his own screen the Governor's face became hard.

'Well, Mr. Rowland?'

'I need an empty shell case immediately, about three feet long and normal width.'

'Oh? Why? Surely you can manufacture one for yourself — ?'

'There isn't time. I must have it now. With it I can stop this interplanetary bombing for good. I've worked out a method which can't fail.'

'I wish I could believe that, Mr. Rowland. Personally I find most of your experiments extremely extravagant and very dangerous — '

'Give me some co-operation, can't you?' Mark demanded. 'I tell you I have the answer and there's no time to waste!'

'He's right, Governor,' Prior put in, angling into view on the screen. 'I've just been a witness of his experiments.'

'What exactly do you propose doing?' Hillman asked, his tone a little more conciliatory since he knew Prior's scientific reputation.

'It would take too long to explain — and in any case I don't see why I should. I'm keeping the method entirely to myself. Just let me have a shell-case as quickly as possible.'

Hillman shrugged. 'Very well. If it doesn't do any good we can't be in a worse mess than we are at present. I'll send the case round to your place immediately.'

Mark switched off and rubbed his hands. 'This ought to do it, Willard — and then watch my climb back to the heights.'

'Far as I can see, Mark, I don't understand enough to help you with the actual 'energizing' of the Heaviside Layer — but if you wish I can return to Pluto and view what happens to Alpha Minor when you do your boomerang act.'

Mark reflected for a while and then he nodded slowly.

'Yes, that might be a good idea. In fact I have a better one. We'll both go to Pluto and view the results. Once I've done my work with the Heaviside Layer there's nothing more I can do, the bouncing-back will be automatic. You'd better get home now and tell your folks what's coming concerning yourself. Be back here in about six hours' time when we ought to be ready for departure.'

'Right . . . ' Prior headed for the laboratory door and then he hesitated, frowning. 'Say, something just occurs to me.'

'What?'

'When you've done your electrical jiggery-pokery with the Heaviside Layer shall we be able to get through it in an atomic transition journey? We, too, will rebound, won't we?'

'Certainly not. Only solids are affected. Light waves and therefore radio waves will pass through the middle as before. We'll get through without difficulty.'

Prior nodded and went on his way, satisfied. Immediately Mark turned his attention to his magnetic equipment, making alterations in its structure so that it could be comfortably housed in the shell-case when it arrived which was half an hour later. Once this happened he was busy for over two hours, fitting remote control devices, atomic batteries, and a small oddly fashioned but tremendously powerful transmitter.

Altogether, including the fashioning of the remote control equipment which was to guide the 'shell' to the heights, the six hours was about up when he had finished

— and also by this time the night had come and with it the distant and sometimes near concussions of high explosive bombs as they peppered Earth relentlessly in a never-ending stream from faraway Alpha Minor. Mark was perfectly aware of the possibility that he might be blown to pieces before he could throw up the defensive screen, but even so he was calm, ruled by an inner conviction that he would survive to make his greatest contribution ever to scientific skill. Evidently something of the same feeling of immunity must have been governing Willard Prior for he arrived unhurt when the six hours were up, though his expression showed the mental strain he had been — and still was — undergoing.

'Thick as hailstones in the middle of the city,' he said. 'Not so bad on the outskirts. I get the impression that these devils on Alpha Minor have some way of pinpointing our thickly populated areas, though how the devil they do it over such a distance is beyond me.'

'If they are the super scientists they're supposed to be, we'll not understand a single thing they accomplish,' Mark replied briefly. 'I only hope they don't scent in advance what I'm planning to do. Anyway — here it is.'

He indicated the Shell, and continued, 'The electrical equipment is inside it, connected to atomic batteries which will produce the required current to set off the chain reaction in the ions of the Heaviside Layer. These electrodes on the outer side of the Shell are connected to the transmitter, by which the required energy will be 'radiated' into the Heaviside Layer. It's as simple as that — so here we go.'

Mark pulled a switch and a half section of the laboratory roof slid back, leaving the naked sky, misty with stars. There was the possibility that at any moment screaming death might hurl itself from the heights — but none came near even though there were the sounds of distant whinings and the sky lighted up transiently at the frictional passage of one of the missiles of destruction.

Turning, Mark switched on the small rocket-recoil motor at the base of the

Shell, to give it its initial start. Almost instantly it shot upwards from its tiny ramp and vanished in a cloud of sparks through the open roof. After that the radio equipment took control, the meters showing the Shell's steady climb. Silent, his eyes fixed on the needle, Prior watched the altitude increase.

One mile — two miles — On and on, higher and higher. Ten miles. A bomb dropped somewhere close and the laboratory swayed. Mark remained tensely at his post, his face drawn and sweating with strain.

'Fifteen miles,' he breathed. 'Still she goes. Sixteen — seventeen.'

The needle still crept. Eighteen — twenty. At twenty-five, at which height the Shell must be well within the Heaviside Layer, Mark snapped another switch which would automatically release the energy from his device. Then he stood silent, looking about him.

The whistle and concussion of bombs was still noticeable, a fact which brought alarm to Prior's face.

'Mark — they're still getting through! It

doesn't work. I told you that you hadn't enough power!'

'Mathematics never lie,' Mark retorted. 'Give the ions time to build up their reaction. It may take an hour.'

He turned aside, dismissing the matter from his mind. For the moment he had done all he could: the rest was up to immutable scientific law. Instead he busied himself with the transition equipment, carefully adjusting the return control. Prior watched him, at the same time listening to remote concussions.

'That should fix that,' Mark said finally. 'I can risk an automatic return control when our objective is no further than Pluto — but to Alpha Minor would demand somebody on the watch. Now — how are we doing?'

He glanced at the clock. Forty-five minutes had passed. 'I haven't heard anything for the last five minutes,' Prior said, his eyes round in wonder.

'Good. Seems to be working. My shell must have fallen back to Earth long ago, its energy discharged — ' Mark turned to the visiphone and switched on. He hardly expected a reply from Governor Hillman, assuming he had probably been blown up — but Hillman appeared on the screen just the same.

'What have you done?' he demanded, almost immediately. 'The reports coming in to me show that the bombs are dropping in decreasing numbers. It's a miracle!'

'I told you it would be,' Mark replied coldly. 'In an hour no bombs at all will fall — or ever again from anywhere. The perfect resistance field has been created. No invader will ever reach us either, no solid one, anyhow. Only radiation can ever get through or have an effect henceforth — and I'll see to it that the world knows later that I devised it. I've no time to explain more. I've things to do.'

Mark switched off and motioned to the magnet area; then he followed Prior into it and snapped on the current. Almost immediately the blank darkness of transition fell upon them both — and when objects again made themselves evident around them they beheld the familiar Plutonian observatory with its huge viltex glass dome bare to the blazing stars and eternal void.

Mark waited a second or two for the fogs of the transition to clear and then he hurried to the huge mirror underneath the immense reflector. At the moment it was dark, its surface covered with velvet-pile, nor was the reflector working.

'Hurry up, man!' Mark snapped, as Prior came over to him. 'We want to be seeing something — Some of the shells have probably already got back to Alpha Minor.'

Prior began to busy himself with the telescope whilst Mark stood gazing through the dome into the endless stars. His attitude, and the constant working of his fingers, showed just how much his emotions were ruling him.

'Right!' Prior exclaimed finally. 'Here we are!' The motors of the reflector hummed and the instrument turned slightly; mirroring everything on the polished mercuroid surface beneath the lenses. Stars in their multimillions swept into view, followed by a dark area, and then an apparent binary star.

'Alpha Centauri,' Prior explained. 'And Proxima Centauri very close to it. You can't see Minor, of course, because it is dark.'

'Once those bombs land back it won't be,' Mark muttered. 'Hell, Willard, I've never felt so keyed up in all my life as I am at this moment.'

Seconds passed into minutes, until at length — taking into account the time taken in making the transition from Earth — and hour and a half had passed. But the black area where Alpha Minor lay remained black.

Mark sighed. 'Well, even if the bombs don't explode when they land back home they'll at least show the master-minds that it's no use sending any more.'

'Don't you believe it,' Prior shook his head dismally. 'If those bombs don't explode, Mark, we've only staved off the trouble for a while. Those superscientists will guess a recoiling defensive screen has been devised and they'll work out something to counteract it — '

'Look!' Mark interrupted, and his hand tightened on the astronomer's arm.

Prior did not speak, and no further words from Mark were necessary either. For a single pinpoint of light had appeared some distance to the left of Alpha Centauri, and with the passing seconds it kindled more brightly — presently assuming a deep, eye-searing brilliance which made Prior turn away and rest his gaze on quieter scenes.

But Mark did not move. Fascinated, grinning with triumph, he watched the blaze spread until the planet that had been Alpha Minor had all the effulgence of a first magnitude star. It even began to outshine Alpha Centauri itself after a while, a fact that caused Mark to frown a little in surprise. Then the possible truth dawned upon him. The bombs that had been hurled back to their starting point had not only exploded, but they had probably detonated thousands of others which were stored ready for use. In consequence a holocaust must be raging throughout that entire distant planet, perhaps even consuming it.

'That,' Mark murmured, as at last the blinding light began to wane, 'should teach them a lesson they will never forget! Possibly their entire civilization was destroyed, Willard. And the Earth is safe! Could there possibly be a better omen for my reaching out into the Universe? I have already destroyed ruthless enemies.'

'Yes — true enough,' Prior admitted, though inwardly he was somewhat horror-stricken at the thoroughness of Mark's reprisal. 'Obviously, the light-waves generated from the bombs were not of the normal order.'

Mark did not answer. He had a curiously blank look on his face. Then suddenly, without the least warning, his face contorted under some unimaginable pain and he crashed to the observatory floor. Instantly Prior rushed to him, examining him quickly. There were no heart or pulse-beats. Mark was dead.

Prior could not believe it — but there the fact was. Nor was there anything he could do about it until the reverse action on the transition equipment operated; then he and the body of Mark were both automatically returned to Earth and

Mark's laboratory and a medical expert was called.

The medical expert said syncope; but the answer was much more scientific than that. In a post mortem, an anatomical physicist discovered that Mark had died because of peculiar radiations passed through his eyes into his brain. The radiations of the mystery bombs, hurled across space with their equally unorthodox light-waves, had had a direct effect on delicate human tissue, and Mark's prolonged gazing at the source of them had killed him.

Such was the ironic truth. In destroying those who had retaliated at his insane ambition he had also destroyed himself, but not before he had saved Earth from any further ill effects — for from the night when a mysterious new 'star' blazed out transiently near Alpha Centauri not another bomb fell on Earth.

The screen remained in position in the Heaviside Layer because it had become an integral part of it, balanced now by the preponderant electrical charge of Earth itself. It had become, by popular acclaim,

Rowland's Layer, replacing that discovered by Kenelly and Heaviside.

Transition journeys to other worlds — in the System only — would continue because the Layer was no barrier to them; but space machines could neither leave Earth nor come to it, which was perhaps an indirect means of insuring that Earth could never be attacked, from no matter what source in the void an invasion might one day come.

Mark Rowland had justified himself in the end, yes, but even in destroying the results of his own ambition he had destroyed himself.

THE END

CLIMATE INCORPORATED
THE FIVE MATCHBOXES
EXCEPT FOR ONE THING
BLACK MARIA, M.A.

We do hope that you have enjoyed reading this large print book.

Did you know that all of our titles are available for purchase?

We publish a wide range of high quality large print books including:
Romances, Mysteries, Classics
General Fiction
Non Fiction and Westerns

Special interest titles available in large print are:
The Little Oxford Dictionary
Music Book, Song Book
Hymn Book, Service Book

Also available from us courtesy of Oxford University Press:
Young Readers' Dictionary
(large print edition)
Young Readers' Thesaurus
(large print edition)

For further information or a free brochure, please contact us at:
Ulverscroft Large Print Books Ltd.,
The Green, Bradgate Road, Anstey,
Leicester, LE7 7FU, England.
Tel: (00 44) **0116 236 4325**
Fax: (00 44) **0116 234 0205**

Other titles in the
Linford Mystery Library

DEATH OF A COLLECTOR

John Hall

It's the 1920s. Freddie Darnborough, popular man about town, is invited to a weekend at Devorne Manor. But the host, Sir Jason, is robbed and murdered hours after Freddie's arrival. However, one of the guests is a Detective Chief Inspector. An odd coincidence? The policeman soon arrests a suspicious character lurking in the shrubbery. But Freddie alone believes the man to be innocent. And so, to save an innocent man from the gallows, Freddie himself must find the real murderer.

SHERLOCK HOLMES AND THE GIANT'S HAND

Matthew Book

Three of the great detective's most singular cases, mentioned tantalisingly briefly in the original narratives, are now presented here in full. The curious disappearance of Mr Stanislaus Addleton leads Holmes and Watson ultimately to the mysterious 'Giant's Hand'. What peculiar brand of madness drives Colonel Warburton to repeatedly attack an amiable village vicar? Then there is the murderous tragedy of the Abernetty family, the solving of which hinges on the depth to which the parsley had sunk into the butter on a hot day . . .

EXCEPT FOR ONE THING

John Russell Fearn

Many criminals have often believed that they'd committed the 'Perfect Crime', and blundered. Chief Inspector Garth of Scotland Yard is convinced that modern science gives the perfect crime even less chance of success. However, Garth's friend, scientist Richard Harvey, believes he can rid himself of an unwanted fiancée without anyone discovering what became of the corpse. Yet though he lays a master-plan and uses modern scientific methods to bring it to fruition, he makes not one but several mistakes . . .

TIDE OF DEATH

E. C. Tubb

England was starving when cheap power could have saved her . . . power that would have been available if the League of Peace had not forbidden atomic research . . . But two scientists ignore the ban and launch an experiment. However, the experiment succeeds too well: it gets out of hand, spreading a tide of black death across the country, and threatens the whole planet. Neil Hammond, a secret agent for the League of Peace, is sent to investigate, and uncovers a terrifying secret . . .